JUSTICE EARNED

JUSTICE EARNED

VALERIE'S ELITES BOOK 4

JUSTIN SLOAN   P.T. HYLTON   MICHAEL ANDERLE

LMBPN

DISRUPTIVE IMAGINATION

To Family, Friends and
Those Who Love
To Read.
May We All Enjoy Grace
To Live The Life We Are
Called.

— Michael

LMBPN Publishing
PMB 196, 2540 South Maryland Pkwy
Las Vegas, NV 89109

First US edition, November 2017
Version 1.04, September 2021

PROLOGUE

VURUGU SYSTEM, LOLACK'S SHIP

Tenowk worked the connection, collaborating with Aranaught in his mind to reach out and catch a glimpse of what they might be up against. He connected the last wire, closed his eyes, and felt the surge of heat. Waves of energy pulsated through him, and he was mentally taken there—large ships, incoming. Unthinkable ships, like blown glass distorted by a storm, but crafted of alien metals. He was in the largest.

This enemy—this figure he couldn't clearly see or name—stood at the helm of this massive destroyer, plugging in and speaking as he did so.

"We have waited long for Lolack to rear his head," the figure said, moving more cables and wires. For him this was an art form; a ritual he clearly had deep respect for. "No more wasting time conquering other star systems—not now that we've found you again, old friend."

A moment passed as the figure glanced around—aware

1

of a presence that should not be there, perhaps. As if a fog around him had dissipated, he became more visible: a shadowy form connected to his ship with thick cables. A helmet hid his features, and no face was visible under it— only darkness.

And then it was over, the figure returning to his ritual.

"It won't be long now," he said, sliding his hands into two conduits on the bridge of his ship. He turned, and his glowing green eyes stared through Tenowk as he traveled through space and time.

He stopped at the edge of a planet on fire. The metal of nearby ships pulled back from the flames as if alive, but he strode past all this. He approached the crest of a hill, below which small domes were cracked, destroyed, craters around them from the blast damage.

He held up a hand and twisted it, and everything moved backwards. The domes were in good shape, the fire and craters and scorched earth gone.

Even *he* was gone, replaced instead by a young Norrul —a male clad only in a loincloth, his skin a thick carapace that almost appeared metal.

He was running toward two figures who were trying to reach him. As the image started to fade, Tenowk could just barely make out the forms of two females. Presumably a wife and daughter?

The explosion hit before they could reach each other, and with a jolt they were pulled out of the vision—and were now back in the figure's ship.

He almost collapsed, this figure, but was held up by the wires and cables that connected his body to the ship.

"Every...time..." he muttered. "It's never...enough." He

regained his composure, standing tall. "Not yet. Not until I've had my day."

"And when we get there… What then, sir?" an almost normal but slightly computerized voice asked.

"Kill them all," the figure replied. "All but this outsider, this 'Prime Enforcer.' She will join us. She will fight for the greater good. For true *justice*."

CHAPTER ONE

SWARTHIAN EXTENDED DETENTION ENVIRONMENT (SEDE)

Gara Grayhewn stepped out her front door at the same time she did every morning. She stood on her porch for a moment observing the house-like structures around her, many of whose residents also stood outside. Most were Skulla or Pallicons, though some had been genetically modified so drastically that it was difficult to identify their races.

A casual observer might think this was a normal neighborhood instead of a cellblock in the star system's most secure prison.

Gara had been incarcerated on SEDE for nearly thirty years, and sometimes she forgot it was a prison too—but those moments didn't last long. And they hadn't come at all since her son Kalan been brought back a little over a month before.

Since then her every waking thought had been dedicated to one thing: getting Kalan out of SEDE…again.

These last weeks had been both a gift and a curse. She'd relished this time spent with the son she'd thought she'd never see again. She'd marveled at his tales of adventures on far-off planets (playing especially close attention whenever he mentioned that cute human, Bob). At the same time, she'd wanted nothing more than to help him escape as quickly as possible. He didn't belong here. She'd rather see him free than be with him in prison.

So far Kalan and his Shimmer friend Wearl had made thirteen attempts to escape, but all had been unsuccessful.

Today they'd make their fourteenth.

Across the walkway, a guy was glaring at her. He was a Skulla—a heavily modded one. He'd been a product of the experiments of the being who had called himself "the Bandian." This false Bandian had ruled the system for a time, until Kalan and his new friends had broken the rightful leader out of SEDE and defeated him.

The Skulla's name was Zoras. He'd given Gara some trouble over the years, but this morning would be different. He nodded slightly, and she saw the hint of a smile in his eyes. He was ready.

Gara lifted a small handheld mirror, angling it so that the reflected light shot toward the starboard end of the cellblock. That was the signal.

As soon as her mirror flashed, everyone sprang into action.

Zoras was the first to move. He barreled down the steps and charged along the walkway, heading to portside. He looked ridiculous. His genetic modifications had made him absurdly muscular, almost as wide as he was tall. Watching him run was so mesmerizing and strange that for a moment Gara forgot to begin her part of the plan.

She recovered quickly from the odd sight, though, and took off down the walkway in the opposite direction.

Gara didn't see Zoras reach his target, but she heard the impact when he slammed his massive body against one of the guard towers. Then she heard a series of smaller impacts—Zoras' Skulla friends hitting the guard tower.

Trying to ignore thoughts of what was happening behind her, Gara fixed her eyes on her own target: another guard tower.

The guard towers in SEDE were strange circular buildings that stood twenty-feet tall, giving the guards a bird's eye view of the walkways throughout the cellblocks. How the Shimmer guards got up into those towers was a mystery to Gara. There were no stairs or ladders, only a ledge no more than an inch wide that spiraled up the buildings' sides.

When she'd asked Wearl how the guards got up there, the Shimmer had simply answered, "We walk." Which hadn't been super-helpful.

The other problem with the guard towers was that it was impossible to tell if they were occupied. For all Gara knew they were attacking empty towers right now, which would sort of lessen the effect they were going for.

As she neared her objective, she was relieved to see Palli-cons gathering at the bottom. She hadn't been sure they would come through on this, so seeing them eased her mind. It hadn't been difficult to convince Zoras and his Skulla to participate in this plan, since they liked to cause trouble.

Anything they could do to throw a wrench in the normal workings of the ship...they were game. The Pallicons were a bit more practical. She'd needed to negotiate with them.

After going back and forth for nearly a week, she'd finally made them an offer they hadn't outright refused: the pistol she kept hidden in exchange for their help. They'd scratched their chins thoughtfully, but hadn't committed one way or another.

Judging by the fact that they were gathered at the bottom of the tower, they were accepting.

The Pallicons shifted, changing their normally lanky forms into a series of angled ridges almost like steps, then climbing onto each other's shoulders.

They were forming a staircase for her with their bodies.

Gara reached them just as they finished and she didn't break her stride. She raced up the living staircase, hoping her pounding feet weren't causing them too much pain. Grayhewns weren't the lightest creatures.

When she reached the top of the stairs, her heart sank. It wasn't quite tall enough.

She gritted her teeth. Zoras, the other Skulla, and the Pallicons had all put themselves on the line for this. More importantly, Kalan was counting on her.

When her foot reached the top step, she pushed off hard and leaped into the air, stretching her arm as far upward as possible. Her fingers touched the edge of the platform.

She grasped it, praying her grip would hold. Thankfully, it did.

Hanging there by one hand, she looked toward the starboard side of the cellblock and a smile appeared on her face.

The gate opened at the end of the block. Though she couldn't see them, she knew Shimmer reinforcements were arriving to deal with the sudden attacks on their guard towers.

Excellent.

As she pulled herself up Gara took one last look toward the gate, hoping to catch a glimpse of Kalan. If all went well, this would be her last chance to see him—hopefully ever. She'd never leave this prison, and if there was any fairness in the universe, *he* would never return.

She didn't spot him; all she saw were the deep shadows where he must be hiding.

She turned her attention back to her situation.

She climbed to her feet, observing the cellblock that had been her home for so long from this high angle for the first time. Then she turned to the apparently empty platform and clenched her fists.

She'd never hit a Shimmer in all her years on SEDE, but that was about to change.

"All right, which of you invisible bastards wants a piece of me first?"

She braced herself for the fight she knew was about to come, a smile on her face and hope for her son blazing in her heart.

"Now?" Kalan asked in a whisper.

"Not yet. Keep your pants on." Wearl paused. "Well, not literally."

They crouched in the shadows, Wearl watching as the Shimmer guards rushed past. Kalan tried to be patient. It would take a few moments after the last guard was through for the mechanical gate to shut, Wearl had observed. The entrance was watched by two guards on the other side of the gate, of course, but with the chaos in the cellblock, Kalan and Wearl were hoping to slip through and take them out.

Since the alarms were already blaring, there was no reason to fear the guards sounding them. Kalan and Wearl just had to take them out before they passed along the message that two prisoners were on the loose.

It still amazed Kalan how much of the prison's security was dependent on the fact that the guards were invisible. Even though they knew Wearl was a prisoner, she would still be able to exploit the weaknesses inherent in the system.

Wearl and Kalan had proven that again and again. In thirteen escape attempts, they'd managed to make it out of the cellblock ten times.

Unfortunately for them SEDE was a massive spaceship, so getting out of the cellblock was only the beginning. Things got decidedly tougher after that.

There were only three possible ways off SEDE. One, gain control of the ship and fly it to a planet or space station, then escape. This method seemed impossible, since they'd need to retain control of the ship for days or weeks, depending on how close they were to an inhabited planet. They had tried this method once, and it hadn't gone well.

Two, get a ride. This could be accomplished by sneaking aboard one of the supply ships that occasionally met up with SEDE, or by having an ally pick them up. Unfortunately there was no way to know when the supply ships would arrive, and no way to communicate with allies who might be in the system where SEDE was currently flying.

The third possible method was the one they were trying today.

"Now," Wearl whispered.

Kalan didn't need to be told twice. He dashed for the gate just as it began to slide closed. As he reached it he turned sideways, angling his big body through the gap just before the gate slammed shut with a clang.

"Where?" he shouted as he ran.

Wearl immediately answered, "Five yards, ten o'clock."

Kalan drew his fist back as he sprinted, then let it fly, punching to his left at about his ten o'clock. He felt a satisfying crunch as his fist connected with an invisible face.

"Got him in one," Wearl shouted.

Kalan heard a struggle in the apparently empty corridor, so he waited. He'd worked with Wearl long enough to know she'd take care of business, and that she'd ask for help if she needed it.

After another moment, there was a loud *crack* and something hit the ground. Then Wearl's voice said, "Okay, let's go."

Kalan took one last look over his shoulder. Through that gate were the beings he'd grown up with. Some had been his friends. Some had been his enemies. But all of them had risked a beatdown or worse so he had a chance to escape.

It brought a lump to his throat.

Not that long ago, he would have refused their help. He would have thought letting them make a sacrifice for him meant he was weak, and he would have insisted on doing it alone.

Then he'd met Valerie. And Robin. And, stars help him, *Bob*. He'd learned a lot from these humans, but the most valuable thing he'd learned was the necessity of teamwork. Asking for help still didn't come easily to him, but he'd begun to understand how much could be accomplished by a group—even a group of convicts like those back in the cellblock.

They'd given him his chance. Now he had to make the most of it.

He followed the sound of Wearl's footsteps as she made her way down the corridor. After so many failed attempts he knew his way around the area outside the cellblock pretty well, and each corridor they entered brought up some painful memory. There was the spot where he'd been hit in the head with a baton while trying to make it to the flight deck. And there was where six Shimmers had dogpiled him while he was headed for the guards' sleeping quarters.

Ah, memories.

Today Wearl was leading them down a series of lightly-traveled corridors. This was a less direct route to their destination, but it would help them avoid any guards rushing to the cellblock to quell the prisoner uprising.

"Almost there," Wearl called to him. "We just need to—"

Her words cut off mid-sentence in a choking sound. Kalan didn't need to see Shimmers to realize they'd been discovered.

"Three o'clock," Wearl ground out.

Kalan threw a hard jab to his direct right and hit a Shimmer in the face.

"Nine o'clock!"

He struck with his left elbow, driving it sideways into another guard.

"Eleven!"

He threw another jab, but this one met empty air. Kalan staggered forward, carried by his own momentum.

"I said eleven!" Wearl shouted. "That was ten!"

Kalan punched again, aiming at his ten o'clock, but it was too late. Rough hands grabbed him, pushing him forward and forcing him to the ground. When they had him on his stomach, they pressed his face forward so his left cheek was flat against the ground.

"All right, you got us," Kalan growled. "Take it easy."

There was no answer as they wrestled his arms behind his back and bound his hands. Something sharp, probably a knee, was driven hard into his back.

Kalan squeezed his eyes shut. He couldn't believe they'd been caught so quickly. He'd let Wearl down. He'd let himself down. He'd let his mother down.

He'd let Valerie down.

She was still out there fighting for justice while he was locked in this flying tomb, and it was driving him crazy. He was one of Valerie's Elites. He belonged out there with her and Bob and Jilla and the rest of the team. Now it would be even longer before he got that chance.

But he'd never give up trying to escape. *Never.*

A Shimmer voice barked in his ear, "You were trying to make it to the hangar, weren't you? Trying to steal another Nim fighter?"

"You have to admit it was pretty effective the first time. Why reinvent the wheel?" There was no use denying it now. This corridor led directly to the fighter bay.

"You're a moron. That never would have worked. We've redesigned the kill switches. You can't fly out unless you have direct authorization from the Flight Deck.

Kalan and Wearl had figured out a workaround for that problem, but he wasn't about to give the Shimmers *that* piece of information.

"Can we go back to our cellblock now?" Kalan asked. "Or are you going to throw us in isolation for a few days again?"

The Shimmer chuckled, and his hot breath tickled Kalan's ear. "Neither. We're taking you to see the captain."

The confident smile melted from Kalan's face, and he went cold.

CHAPTER TWO

VURUGU SYSTEM, UNKNOWN PLANET

Waters lapped the side of Commander Lolack's ship, and Valerie watched the ebb and flow as she contemplated her next move. She and Robin had climbed to the edge of one of the turrets to get away and have a moment to think. They'd landed on a fringe planet after entering the Vurugu system—the same system Tol occupied—and soon Valerie would find out why.

"It won't be easy," Valerie said, glancing back.

Robin stood behind her, leaning against the base of the massive gun mount with her arms crossed. "What won't?"

"I don't know yet. But whichever way we go, it won't be easy." She pushed herself up, then paced, hands behind her back. "Kalan gave himself up, but he's part of the team now. We can't leave him."

"He's on a prison ship," Robin pointed out. "We might not have much of a choice."

Valerie glared. "I wouldn't leave *you* there, and I believe I could say the same of you."

Robin nodded at that.

"So the same applies here," Valerie stated. "He's one of us now."

"Yes. We go after him."

"On the other hand, we have numerous enemies incoming," Valerie pointed out. "The fleet will soon be under siege. If the fleet could find a prime defensive spot—"

"A prime spot for the Prime Enforcer."

"*Really?*" Valerie turned to her friend and laughed.

Robin shrugged.

"Right. The point is, we need to ensure victory here. It's not just about us, it's about the entire Etheric Federation." Valerie sighed. "Sometimes it sucks, having to think of more than just ourselves."

"There's good news in all this," another voice said. Admiral Lolack was easily maneuvering his way up to them, but he stopped to pull Arlay up behind him. In stark contrast to her blue skin and tentacles instead of hair, he was tall and willowy with orange skin, like the rest of his kind.

Valerie turned to him with an embarrassed grin. "I didn't mean we'd abandon you, just to be clear."

"I wouldn't worry about it," he said with a wave of his hand. "We have Tenowk—the IAI—and the rest of my fleet is coming. The worrisome part is trying to figure out when the enemy fleet will arrive, and what damage they might to be able to do before we can get to them."

"If the Etheric Federation—" Robin started, but Lolack held up a hand.

"There's no way they'd reach us in time, and everything I've heard leads me to believe they're quite busy with their own issues. However, I think there's a way you can help... yet again."

"We can't just abandon Kalan," Valerie stated.

Arlay grinned, nudging Lolack as she said, "See, didn't I tell you? Loyal to a fault."

"Not a fault in *my* book. This is what we need." Lolack stared into Valerie's eyes a moment longer, weighing her, and said, "There's a mission, and maybe finding and recovering your friend will be part of it."

"How so?"

He stepped forward, looking into the sky, where already some of his ships were preparing to move.

"There's a planet without a local populace not so far off. It was set up in my day as a fallback position. Essentially, the Minas Tirith of space..." He waited, grinning, then frowned. "You two don't get the reference?"

Valerie shook her head and glanced at Robin, who shrugged.

He sighed. "Why'd I spend all that time boning up on the literature and films of Earth, if the only two Earthers I've met have no idea what I'm talking about? Suffice it to say, the location is the ultimate defensive position. Problem? We don't know exactly where it is, only the direction. We can start moving, and hope you succeed."

"Wonderful. Your fate would be in our hands?" Robin asked with a chuckle.

"The fate of this galaxy," Valerie corrected.

"Nothing new there."

Arlay nodded at the two, who were standing tall. "So, you're in?"

"Aren't we always?" Valerie assured her. "But how's this tie into Kalan?"

"That's up to you," Lolack replied. "When we go to my office, I'll show you the information we have. It's not a lot, but your boy Kalan knows his way around. If he's really a Bandian, he might be able to leverage it and... It's part of the puzzle, really. You'll see."

"You're saying we might not need him, or he might be integral to saving the galaxy?"

Arlay laughed. "Sounds about right."

Lolack nodded, then motioned them to follow him. "Honestly, we're not sure. It might be that you can find it without him, and much faster. Breaking him out of the most secure prison in the known universe—that could take a lifetime, and our lives might not be very long if you go that route."

He paused until they had all gone below, then moved through the hatch. Inside the ship, everyone was busy with the checks and processes required to get her into the air. Apparently Lolack was serious about getting off the ground ASAP.

"I'm not one to micromanage," Lolack told them as they crossed the main deck and headed toward his office. "You've proven you can get the job done, so I'll simply ask that you do this one and save our asses."

"And what'll *you* be doing?" Robin asked, earning a glare from Valerie.

"I don't think she meant that to come out as it did," Valerie interjected.

Lolack's grin was still there, but his eyes narrowed. "I'll be leading my fleet, pulling the rest of the ships together, and preparing for a battle that could very well decimate us. Even if I do my job right I still expect at least half the fleet to be lost, so," his smile faded, "don't act like my job will be easy."

"Sorry, sir," Robin replied, knowing when to check herself.

When they entered Lolack's office, they gathered around the holodisplay of the current star system. A few other star systems were represented by red dots.

"We've entered the Vurugu System," he started. "Our destination is somewhere within this star system, though we're not sure where." He tapped the screen, causing it to zoom in tighter. "The Silahu Corporation operates out of Rhol. They've supplied half the weapons I've ever run across, if not more. Someone from the Vurugu system was working with them on this secret weapon—this star defense system—and they'll have the answers we need."

Robin sucked in air. "Yeah, Val doesn't have the best history with corporations. They always butt heads."

"Only when they're packaging the blood of my brothers and sisters to sell against their will," Valerie protested.

"I'd say that's a damn good reason," Arlay chimed in. "Considering that these guys supply both good and bad, you might end up finding some morally ambiguous shit."

"Might, might not," Lolack agreed, "but stay focused on the mission."

Valerie nodded, then turned at a sound from the door. A young female stuck her head in and stated, "Admiral Lolack, we're prepared for departure."

"Thank you." He turned to Valerie. "The *Grandeur* is on board?"

"It is."

"Then proceed," he told the female, who bowed her head before exiting.

"We'll go as a group and let you off when we approach Rhol so that—"

"Sir!" The female was back.

He frowned as he stared at her.

"An attack on our forward ships," she added when she realized that was all she was going to get.

"Dammit, already?" he exclaimed, swiping a hand across the board on the wall to turn it into a display. He chose from several of the cameras on the ships already up there, and they were able to see enemy ships swooping down and attacking as turrets fired back. "Get us up there," he shouted. "*NOW!*"

CHAPTER THREE

SWARTHIAN EXTENDED DETENTION ENVIRONMENT (SEDE)

For the first time in as long as Kalan could remember, he was nervous.

He'd thought he was ready for anything; any punishment they could come up with. After fourteen escape attempts, he'd assumed they were going to raise the stakes. He'd considered torture, isolation, maybe even cutting off a hand. But he hadn't considered this.

The first story Kalan remembered hearing about the captain was probably the most famous. There weren't a lot of them. Every convict in SEDE knew there was a captain in charge of the Shimmers, and that he was the only being who knew the flight path SEDE would take. But little else was known about him…other than this story.

The way Kalan had heard it, it had happened about twenty-five years ago, shortly before he was born. A cellblock near the stern of the ship had decided they'd had enough of the Shimmers guarding them and launched a full-scale riot, killing some of the Shimmers and forcing the others to retreat. They'd managed to hold their cell-block for nearly a week.

Then the captain had shown up.

No one knew exactly what he'd said to the leaders of the revolt, but somehow he'd convinced them to let him inside the cellblock. He'd gone in alone and unarmed, but had quickly taken the leader's shank and stabbed him with it. Then he'd unlocked the gates and let in his guards.

After the riot had been quelled and all the rioters had been subdued, the captain had calmly and deliberately walked through the cellblock and shot every male, female, and child in the head. He'd then ordered the cellblock dismantled and everything in it tossed out an airlock.

Kalan's logical mind rejected the story, realizing that if no one but the guards and the captain had survived, there would be no one to spread the story—and yet he couldn't shake feeling he'd had when he'd first heard the tale at five years old.

Even though the captain was shrouded in mystery, everyone knew one fact about him: when the captain got involved, people died.

Kalan glanced at the spot he knew Wearl was standing. "You okay?"

"Okay? I'm *more* than okay. I've been wanting to talk to this bastard for years."

Kalan raised an eyebrow. "Really?"

"Oh, yes. He has far too much influence on the

Shimmer culture. His brutal recruitment process is part of what causes so much infighting among us. That's not good management."

"I didn't know you had such strong feelings about management techniques."

"Of course I do. I'm not a savage."

They were waiting in a small metal room, their hands bound. Kalan had no idea how long they'd been in there, but his stomach told him it had been a while.

They sat in silence for a few more minutes before the door slid open with a clang.

A disembodied voice said, "Get up. He's ready for you."

Wearl sighed. "You're lucky you can't see Shimmers, Kalan. This one's really ugly."

"Shut up and move, traitor."

Kalan got to his feet and took a deep breath. A hand touched his back, and he allowed it to guide him down a short corridor that led to a large corridor, and finally to a set of double doors.

The guard behind Kalan paused at the entrance. "This is it." The doors opened and the guard spoke again in a softer voice. "Good luck."

"What, you're not coming with us?" Wearl asked.

The guard chuckled. "No way. You're on your own in there. The captain wanted to speak to you two, not me. Thank the stars."

Kalan stood straight and tall. He'd faced down the Wandarby fleet, and a crazy Bandian cyborg. He wouldn't let this captain intimidate him. He walked confidently into the captain's chambers.

The room was about as stark a contrast as was possible to the sterile metal corridors. There was metal here too, but it was finely polished silver and brass. Most of the furniture, including the large desk that dominated the room, was made of a beautiful greenish wood Kalan had never seen before.

Captain Tuttle was tapping away on a screen embedded in his desktop when they entered. He didn't look up.

As he stood silently waiting, Kalan's anger grew. This guy already had them over a barrel. He was just flexing now, drawing out the misery.

"You wanted to see us, Captain?" Kalan tried to keep the growl out of his voice when he said it.

The captain held up a finger and continued tapping at the screen with his other hand.

Kalan was about to tell him where he could shove that finger when the male finally spoke.

"Sorry about that. Very rude of me. Thanks for waiting."

The captain looked up with a wide, friendly smile on his face. He was a Skulla, but more lightly tattooed than most Kalan had met. His eyes were a pale-green color that perfectly matched the wood of the desk.

He looked first at Kalan, then glanced at the empty spot next to the Bandian.

"Kalan. Wearl. I've been looking forward to meeting you."

Kalan wasn't sure how to respond to that. "Well, I've been here since the day I was born, minus a few years recently. You could have stopped by to say hi anytime."

The captain chuckled. "That's right. It's not exactly uncommon for a sabie to come back here. Recidivism, they call that in the correctional business. But most aren't dragged back by a fleet of angry Shimmers."

"They felt that I had besmirched their honor." Kalan spoke slowly and carefully. Tuttle wasn't acting at all like Kalan had expected. Clearly this was some sort of trap to make them feel at ease before bringing the hammer down on them, but Kalan wasn't falling for it. He didn't relax a single muscle. "I suppose I besmirched your honor too, Captain."

Tuttle waved the thought away. "Nonsense. I don't go in for all that honor stuff. I'm a businessman." He gestured to the chairs in front of the desk. "Please, have a seat."

Kalan hesitated, but then sat down.

Wearl seemed to have none of his misgivings. "Sure thing, Captain," she said cheerfully.

Kalan briefly wondered whether Tuttle could hear Wearl, but then he realized the Skulla worked with Shimmers all day every day. They were his only employees. He *must* be able to hear them.

The captain leaned back in his seat. "So...fourteen breakout attempts?"

Kalan gritted his teeth. Here it came. Now Tuttle would drop the nice-guy act and lay down the punishment.

"You know, I have to say I'm impressed." He raised a stubby finger. "Not just at the persistence, but at the ingenuity."

"Thanks," Wearl replied cheerfully.

Tuttle leaned forward. "Having spent most of my adult life on this prison ship, I've given a lot of thought to how I'd escape if I were incarcerated here. I've long thought I'd try to sneak aboard one of the supply ships. Of course, the challenge would be figuring out when the resupply would happen. You'd have to carefully watch the supply of a necessary resource—say water—and figure out how long it generally took between replenishments. Then take your best guess."

Kalan's eyes widened. How did the captain know?

Tuttle looked Kalan in the eye. "I was delighted when you two attempted that exact method. You only miscalculated by one day, you know. It was a close thing."

Now Kalan leaned forward. "Captain, if you don't mind, I think we'd like to find out about our punishment and be on our way."

"Speak for yourself," Wearl interjected. "I want to talk about the Shimmers' working conditions."

Captain Tuttle ignored her comment. His eyes sparkled with genuine delight. "Is that why you thought you were here? To be punished?" He let out a loud belly laugh. "You're already in prison for life. What more can I do? Make your life shittier? What would be the point? As I said, you intrigue me. Here, let me show you something."

Tuttle pushed a button and the screen raised up from his desk, swiveling around so Kalan and Wearl could see it. Then it blinked to life.

Kalan's eyes narrowed at what he saw.

The screen showed black and white footage of Kalan and Bob sneaking through the corridors of SEDE, Sslake close behind them. They made their way into the hangar and began firing at invisible Shimmers.

The image changed, now showing another corridor. This one took longer for Kalan to identify. Then Kalan, Valerie, Robin and the rest of the team ran into view and

Kalan recognized the location. It was the Tol moon base where they'd battled the mechs and robots.

The picture flickered again, and this time Kalan got it right away. It was the battle on Rewot when Kalan and his new Lavkin family had fought the Wandarby cultists. From the angle of the footage and the fact that it was showing the end of the battle, Kalan guessed it had been taken from one of the Shimmer ships that had come to save the Lavkins in exchange for Kalan surrendering to them.

Then the image disappeared, leaving only the black mirror of the darkened screen.

"That moon base footage was difficult to track down," Tuttle admitted. "I paid too much for it. On the other hand, what else am I going to do with my money?"

Kalan sat in silence. What was Captain Tuttle's game here? What did he really want from them?

As the screen receded back into the desktop Wearl told him, "I'm glad to see you're a fan of our work. I'm happy to sign autographs, but I don't much like stalkers."

The captain chuckled. "I'm not here to stalk or to get autographs. I'm here to offer you a choice."

Kalan frowned. "So there *will* be a punishment. I knew it."

Tuttle shrugged. "Not a punishment exactly, though it *is* true I can't have you trying to break out every three days. My guards have better things to do, and it's really cutting into my overtime budget."

He paused, as if thinking of how to continue.

"I know you two might not see me in the most positive light. Kalan, you probably grew up hating and fearing me, and Wearl, you probably think I'm a cruel boss to your people."

"Accurate assessment," Wearl answered.

"I had good intentions when I got into this job. I took it for one reason, and one reason alone: I believed in justice."

The sincerity with which he said it made Kalan sit up a bit straighter in his chair. *Justice*—the same cause Valerie's Elites fought for every day.

The captain continued, "Back in my early days, I really believed that I could bring criminals here, have them pay a fair price based on what they'd done, and reform them while I was at it."

"You don't believe that anymore?" Kalan asked.

Tuttle shrugged. "I still think it's possible, but I know it's the exception rather than the rule. But I want to do a better job. I want to fight for true justice, for those in here as well as those outside. That's where you two come in."

Kalan waited. If this was all some sort of sales pitch to get him to be a jackboot for this tyrant, there was no way he would buy it. And yet, the Skulla did seem absolutely sincere.

"Here's the choice I mentioned. First option is, I can lock you both in the isolation block for the rest of your lives." He held up a hand. "Like I said, not a punishment. I respect your work, but there has to be a price for so many escape attempts."

The isolation block was where Sslake had been held, and Kalan had seen it firsthand. It wasn't a bad place. Each inmate got a rough approximation of a house to call his or her own. But the isolation... Could Kalan handle spending the rest of his life completely alone, only seeing the prisoner who delivered his food for a few moments each day?

Kalan didn't know what the average lifespan of a Bandian was, but based on the rumors his father had passed to his mother they were a very long-lived people. Kalan could be looking at a few hundred years of solitude.

He wasn't the most extroverted guy in the world, but could he handle having no interpersonal contact? Never seeing his mother, or Wearl, or even that crazy jerk Zoras?

"What's the other option?"

Tuttle folded his hands on the desktop and smiled. "The other option is, you work for me. You fight for justice."

There was a long silence.

Kalan finally spoke. "No way. Wearl can answer for herself, but I'm not doing it."

Tuttle nodded, unsurprised. "May I ask why? As I've already implied, you'd be helping your fellow prisoners."

"Unless helping them means loading them on a ship and flying that ship to freedom, I'm not interested."

"If Kalan's out, so am I," Wearl quickly added. "Besides, I can totally break out of your isolation block. Watch and see if I don't."

Tuttle's smile widened. "Good. I knew you were beings of integrity. I would have been disappointed if you'd accepted my offer right away." He pressed a button, and once again the screen raised out of his desk. "That isn't the end of my pitch. It was just the warm-up. I fully believe that once you've heard the details of the job, you'll change your mind."

As Tuttle explained further, Kalan felt himself leaning

forward, getting caught up in the man's story. Despite himself, he was intrigued.

The opportunity to fight for justice—the kind he'd never had as a kid—was too exciting to pass up immediately. And the more he learned, the more interested he became.

Ten minutes later, Kalan and Wearl accepted the job.

CHAPTER FOUR

VURUGU SYSTEM, LOLACK'S SHIP

Lolack's ship had begun firing on the enemy long before reaching them, thanks to the ship's long-range locking capabilities. The admiral had invited the rest of Valerie's team to join them at the display. They were still very much out of sight, but riding to what could be the last battle of their lives clearly wasn't sitting well with Bob.

His eyes were glued to the screen displaying the distant feed as another ship took a hit. From the way his fingers clutched the armchair, Valerie would almost think he'd never been in a battle before. Of course, she knew that wasn't the case, so it had to be something else.

"You hangin' in there, Bob?" she asked.

He glanced at her, then Jilla, and leaned over. "It's not me I'm worried about."

"Oh?"

"You know me, always looking out for the weak."

"I'll take you out right now," Jilla told him with a glare.

Valerie laughed nervously as she turned back to the display. The ship was moving forward, but it was so large she could almost pretend it wasn't moving at all. Robin was at her side, smiling as her eyes darted across the display.

"What's up with the grin?" Valerie asked.

"If this is all they've got, we have no reason to worry," Robin explained.

"Big 'if' there," Lolack said, turning away from the screen to offer them some alcohol from his home planet. "I'm guessing this is a scouting party—some of their fastest, to see what they're up against. That means small guns, easy to take out...but nothing compared to what's next."

Robin shrugged, still grinning. "Well, at least they're getting their butts kicked for now. Here's hoping it'll last." She raised her glass, then took a swig. Her eyes went all buggy, and Valerie laughed at her face as she forced herself to swallow.

"Tough stuff?" Valerie asked, sniffing the drink. It had an almost squash-like smell.

"Not my style, is all."

"Hey, at least our bodies heal from it," Valerie remarked, downing hers in one gulp. Holy shitstains, that was nastier than eating rotten-orange-covered socks. She did her best not to make a face, but it was clear from Lolack's amused expression that she'd failed.

"Don't worry, it's not like many of mine can keep it down either," he reassured her. "The game is, 'who can show the least amount of discomfort.' You didn't do as badly as your friend here."

"Thanks for telling me the rules *first*." Robin's tone was heavily sarcastic.

"As if you'd stand a chance anyway," Garcia called from the back of the room. He accepted a glass, and gagged just at the smell. "Shit, never mind. Good for you all, but I'm not touching the stuff."

"Garcia, it'll be a huge insult if you don't," Valerie warned him.

"Really?"

"No," Lolack said.

"I meant to me." Valerie grinned. "How dare you?"

Garcia rolled his eyes and passed it to Flynn, who downed his and accepted Garcia's with a smile. "What? It's actually pretty good?"

"For the first time ever," Robin said to him, "you worry me."

"You all should be worried about what's going on," Arlay interjected, pointing to the screens, "instead of playing around."

"Relax." Lolack smiled.

"Excuse me?" She frowned at him as if he'd just thrown the table across the room. "Those are *your* fighters out there."

"And our ship is doing its damage," he explained. "There's not much we can do from here."

She was clearly the kind of leader who was used to being in the trenches with her fighters, while Lolack practiced a more removed style of leadership.

"She has a point, though." Valerie stood and turned to Lolack. "The crew of the *Grandeur* should get going. We're close enough now, right? And you can cover us until we're out of their reach?"

He nodded. "Yes to both."

"Let's get moving, then," Valerie told Robin and the rest of her team, glad to have something to do other than sit around on someone else's ship. Even if they had been in battle, there wasn't much a vampire could do while the ships were shooting each other. But going on-planet or to space stations and tracking down bad guys and strange mysteries, or investigating alien weapons makers and searching for some sort of map? That was where she excelled.

They made their way back through the ship. The main walkways were now empty, since everyone was either at their battlestation or in the viewing room. The *Grandeur* was in the launch bay, fueled and ready to go.

Valerie made for the door and then stopped, noticing a blinking light on the floor. A second came to life next to it, then another, then several more, leading her gaze to the far wall where Tenowk stood in the shadows.

"Leaving without saying good bye?" he asked with a grin.

"Go ahead and get her ready." Valerie waved her team on. "I'll be a sec."

"I wanted to thank you before you go," Tenowk told her as he approached. His robotic face looked better now that they'd concealed the wires and whatnot. "If not for you, I'd be this crazy AI's slave."

"Not so crazy anymore," the female voice of the AI retorted. Aranaught had been corrupt, with plans of taking down the Lost Fleet—Lolack's Fleet—and more, but not after Lolack had worked his tech magic on her.

"Tell that to everyone who sees me talking to myself." Tenowk grinned, then seemed to remember Valerie was there. "Right…thanks. Again. Just, now that I have this kind of cognitive techiness, it's like I'm learning myself all over again. When you're out there, I'm going to keep an eye out. I owe you."

"You don't owe me. Lolack was the one who figured it out."

He nodded. "Him too. Just be careful, and if you ever need anything… Wait…" He held up a hand, closed his eyes, and then opened them as cheering echoed through the ship.

"What was that?" she asked.

"Took over a few of their ships and turned them against their own. I sure wish I could see the looks on their faces. Wait, maybe I can." Again he closed his eyes, this time laughing.

"Take care, Tenowk, and you too, Aranaught."

"Thank you," they answered in unison.

Valerie headed to the ship, boarding to find the others seated and the engines running.

"Let's go find trouble," Valerie suggested, and grinned as Tenowk made an image of the other ships appear on their screen for a moment, then feeds of the enemy running around inside in chaos. "We'll need to see where we're going," Valerie shouted, but couldn't help laughing.

"Good to have him, or her—them—on our side," Garcia commented, nodding to Flynn as the latter got the *Grandeur* moving.

"Too bad he isn't coming with us," Valerie noted. "We have no idea what we're about to ride into."

"That's what makes it so fun," Robin quipped, and Valerie had to agree. Sometimes it was the thrill of it all that kept her going. Mostly, however, it was those at her side.

CHAPTER FIVE

SWARTHIAN EXTENDED DETENTION ENVIRONMENT (SEDE)

"Why does it seem like we spend half our time sneaking around in the corridors of this ship?" Wearl asked.

"Because we do." Kalan chuckled. "Hey, it wasn't *my* fault you got yourself arrested. You didn't have to follow me into prison. You could be hanging out with Valerie and the Elites right now."

"Yes, I'm sure they're having a very peaceful, uneventful time. That sounds just like our Valerie."

Kalan had to admit, the Shimmer did have a point. They had been spending a lot of time in these corridors lately, but this time they were on official prison business. "You been here before?"

"To Cellblock One-Eight-Nine? No. They told us about it in my training program back in the day, though. Said to hope you didn't get assigned there."

"Same with the prisoners. It's the one cellblock you

don't want to be transferred to. People who walk into One-Eight-Nine never walk out again."

"So remind me again why we're doing this?" Wearl asked.

Kalan smiled. "Because we love justice."

"Sure. Just like the captain."

Captain Tuttle's sales pitch had won Kalan over, despite his misgivings about the Skulla's motives. According to Tuttle, Cellblock One-Eight-Nine was the one place he couldn't seem to get under control. The reason was simple: a Pallicon named Nostro.

Cellblock kingpins were common in SEDE—Kalan had seen a dozen of them come and go in his own cellblock during his childhood. They controlled the contraband, and often bullied other inmates. Some were worse than others, but according to Tuttle, Nostro was a whole different type of kingpin. Somehow he'd done the impossible—he'd gotten the guards into his pocket.

The Shimmers had been straightforward with Tuttle about the situation: the one thing they wouldn't do for him was go after Nostro. Unless he wanted every guard in SEDE to quit, he would leave Nostro alone.

Captain Tuttle didn't understand how Nostro had done it, but he was through putting up with the situation. That was where Kalan and Wearl came in. They were to sneak into One-Eight-Nine, capture Nostro, and bring him to Captain Tuttle. If the Shimmers wouldn't give the captain the answers he wanted, maybe the kingpin himself would.

"Tuttle really won you over with that story of his, didn't he?" Wearl asked as they walked.

Kalan shrugged. "A kingpin with total control over the

guards? He could be doing *anything* to the other inmates in his block. What can I say? I don't like bullies."

"So I've noticed."

They reached a metal door marked "189" in tall, blocky white letters. Tuttle had told them this door led to the supply area, from which they should be able to sneak into the cellblock without attracting too much attention. They'd been given a keycard that would open all doors in One-Eight-Nine, but it would automatically deactivate after twelve hours—a safety precaution in case it fell into the wrong hands.

"What about you?" Kalan asked. "The captain's story worked on you too."

"Nah, this just sounded like fun. I bet we'll get to punch somebody."

"Probably more than one somebody, knowing us. Here we go on another dumb adventure."

Kalan took a deep breath and held up the keycard. The reader flashed green, and the metal door slid open.

They stepped into a stockroom. Tall shelving units loaded with crates lined the walls.

Kalan made his way to the other end of the room and peeked through the window built into the door. One-Eight-Nine looked similar to any other cellblock. The cells looked like small homes, except for the doors that locked when the guards pushed a button—just like in Kalan's cellblock. The walkway appeared to be clear, but he wasn't going to take that for granted. "Check it for Shimmers?"

He stepped out of the way, allowing Wearl to look out the window.

"We're good," she said after a moment.

Kalan eased the door open and cautiously stepped into the cellblock. "Now we just have to find Nostro."

They'd gone no more than twenty feet down the walkway when they spotted the boy. He couldn't have been more than five years old, and he stood frozen in the center of the walkway, staring up at them with wide eyes. Kalan could clearly see the sabie tattoo on his arm.

"Crap," Kalan muttered. He tried to make his voice sound friendly when he spoke again. "Hey, there. Are you—"

That was as far as he got before the kid turned and dashed away, disappearing into a cell a little way down the walkway.

"Well, there goes the element of surprise," Wearl quipped lightly.

A moment later, four large Pallicons stepped out of the cell the child had entered. They squinted at Kalan for a moment, then stalked toward him.

"Wearl, if this goes as badly as I think it's about to, I want you to stay out of it," he said quickly. "You're my wild-card. I need to hold you until the time is right to lay you down."

"Did you just say you want to hold me and lay me down?" the Shimmer asked.

"Just do as I say," Kalan ordered.

The four Pallicons reached him, two of them quickly moving to either side to flank him.

The one directly in front of Kalan glared at him. "Who are you, and how the hell did you get in here?"

Kalan said the first thing that came to mind. "That's confidential. I need to talk to Nostro."

"Confidential?" He chuckled. "You want to see Nostro? No problem."

He nodded to his companions on either side of Kalan and the two grabbed Kalan's arms, roughly guiding him down the walkway.

As they took him to the far end of the cellblock Kalan's mind raced, trying to figure out what he'd say to the kingpin when he reached him. Sneaking into a cellblock unseen had been an unlikely proposition, but he hadn't thought it would go badly so quickly.

On the plus side they'd agreed to take him to Nostro, and so far Wearl hadn't attacked them. That was all he could think of for positives.

They stopped at the last cell on the far end of the block. One Pallicon growled, "Wait here," as if Kalan had any choice with the two males holding his arms. The Pallicon walked through the shadowy doorway, and Kalan and the others waited in silence.

A few moments later, a large figure filled the doorway. Kalan couldn't make out his features in the shadows, but from the way the Pallicons holding him tensed he assumed this was Nostro.

"You wanted to see me?" the shadowy figure asked. His voice was low and inarticulate, like his lips couldn't quite form the proper sounds.

Kalan cleared his throat and started to speak. "I was just transferred here, and I—"

The shadowy figure held up a hand, cutting him off. "Let me stop you there. I only allow beings one chance, and you just blew it by lying." He paused a moment, and Kalan got the feeling the shadowy figure was studying him. "I know who you are. I've heard things. You're the Grayhewn —the sabie who broke Sslake out. You got yourself thrown back in here, and have been trying to escape ever since."

There was no use denying it. "Yeah, that's me. Kalan Grayhewn."

"Well, Kalan Grayhewn, I get apprised of any new transfers to the One-Eight-Nine, and I wasn't apprised of you. That means you're here for an unsavory purpose, and I don't allow such things in my block."

"I understand, and I—"

The shadowy figure held up a hand again. "I already told you: I only give one chance, and you blew yours." He turned to the Pallicon next to him. "Take him to the pit."

The figure disappeared back into the house as the Pallicons hauled Kalan away, now holding him even tighter.

"We have to go into the pit for this idiot?" one of the Pallicons holding him complained.

"You heard him." another answered. "Just breathe through your mouth. It'll be fine."

"That smell's gonna stay in my clothes for a week."

"So I'm guessing 'pit' isn't shorthand for 'pleasure pit?'" Kalan asked.

"No, it ain't. Get all your jokes out now, because I promise you won't be laughing in there."

They led Kalan to a doorway at the other end of the block. The lead Pallicon took a deep breath and pulled the door open.

The smell hit Kalan immediately, as did the knowledge of where they were taking him.

All cellblocks had the same basic layout, including a garbage disposal unit at the port end. The disposal generally had a sliding door through which the garbage could be dropped into a containment unit, where it waited to be hauled away.

It appeared Nostro and his crew had made some modifications.

The sliding door had been replaced with a regular door, and a stairway that led down into the garbage pit had been installed.

The extent of the physical changes shocked Kalan. He couldn't believe they'd been able to get away with all this. Not only must Nostro have the guards in his pocket, but he had to have some way to get the materials and equipment needed to make this happen.

"No use delaying the inevitable," one of the Pallicons said with a sigh. He pushed Kalan forward.

If the smell was bad outside the door of the garbage pit, it was much worse once they got inside. The ground squished as Kalan walked, and his feet sank ankle-deep into garbage with every step. Kalan wished Nostro had just given him a beating like a normal kingpin would have.

The Pallicons led him to a wall, shoved his back against it, and locked his wrists into built-in shackles. Apparently he wasn't the first being to get the garbage-pit treatment.

Once he was locked into the shackles, the lead Pallicon's face softened a little. It almost appeared he felt sorry for Kalan.

"Look, I'm not supposed to tell you this, but we'll be back for you in twenty-four hours. Nostro likes to do this to soften people up. Just make sure you're quick with honest answers next time you see him, or you'll be spending a lot more time down here." He started to turn away, but looked back at Kalan. "I'd say you'll get used to the smell, but that would be a lie."

With that, the Pallicons headed up the stairs. As the door shut behind them, the lights went out.

Kalan was alone in the dark in a putrid pit of garbage.

He really didn't like this Nostro guy.

All he needed to do was get through the next twenty-four hours. He could handle that. It wasn't all that long.

He took a deep breath…and immediately regretted it. The foul air filled his lungs, and he started coughing.

Then he heard laughter.

"The Grayhewn doesn't like the taste of our air," a deep male voice said.

A female voice answered, "If I could get out of these shackles, I'd beat him so badly he'd forget all about the air."

Kalan blinked hard in confusion. There hadn't been anyone else down here when the guards had shackled him, and yet they had said they were shackled too.

There was only one explanation. It wasn't that these mysterious beings hadn't been there when the lights were on. It was just that he hadn't been able to see them.

"You're Shimmers," he stated.

There was a long silence, then the female spoke. "You can hear us?"

That confirmed it for Kalan. "Maybe we can help each other. How long have you been down here?"

The male Shimmer scoffed. "*Help* you? After the disgrace you caused our people?"

Kalan grimaced. He'd just about had it with strangers hating him because of who he was or what he'd supposedly done. "You don't have to like me. I'm suggesting—"

"Good, because I *don't* like you. I think I hate you more than I hate Nostro."

"That's saying a lot," the female Shimmer chimed in, "because he *really* hates Nostro."

"That's for sure. He's deceiving every guard in this place. I don't know where he got that fake Borin's Tooth, but it's not fooling me."

"'Borin's Tooth?'" Kalan asked. "What's that?"

The Shimmers were very quiet for a long moment, then one of them spoke again. "You don't need to concern yourself with any of that. You're a prisoner, which means he'll let you out tomorrow, just as his henchman said. Until then, mind your own business."

Kalan sighed. Why did everything in this prison have to be so damn difficult?

He waited there in the silence for what felt like hours. He never really got used to the smell, but the urge to vomit eventually subsided. That was something to be thankful for, he supposed.

He'd almost fallen asleep when a door opened and a brilliant shaft of light cut through the darkness, momentarily blinding him. The door was on the other end of the garbage room from where he'd entered.

Kalan blinked hard, trying to force his eyes to adjust to the light. It couldn't have been a full day already. Was it possible Nostro had changed his mind? That he was going to let him go? Or was he going to kill him?

A hand roughly grabbed his wrist and began unlatching his shackle. "This smell is truly revolting. Even *you* can't make this place sexy."

"Wearl?"

She unlatched his other hand, and he let out a sigh of relief as he rubbed his sore wrists.

"Happy you recognized me. Now, what do you say we get out of this stinkhole and go show Nostro who he's dealing with?"

Kalan grinned. "I like the sound of that just fine."

CHAPTER SIX

PLANET RHOL

Whatever they'd expected, this planet was nothing like it. The rising metal pillars were the most impressive—tall buildings with purple sunlight glimmering off them and faces sticking out to see the *Grandeur* as it flew overhead.

"They've prospered from the success of Silahu," Jilla snarled, practically spitting. "Meaning, from the money used to buy weapons that have cost both sides millions of lives over the years. These people live on blood money."

"And that is why you'll be staying to guard the ship," Valerie replied. "Too close to the issue."

"Too *close*?" Jilla scoffed, turning away but not saying anything more on the subject.

"What *is* all this?" Garcia asked.

"I think it's where they live," Flynn replied, pulling up zoomed-in images of the beings looking out the windows at them. The locals weren't very different from Skulla, except that instead of tattoos they wore heavy metal piercings shaped like the towers they lived in.

At the outskirts of the tower complex, the land transformed from rust-colored bushes to ground that looked like desert but shone as if reflecting the sunlight. It was like endless clay in all directions.

"I've never seen anything like it," Robin said, staring in awe.

"It's not that special," Jilla argued.

"How do they make the towers, or do they just form that way?" Garcia asked.

Even Jilla didn't have the answer to that one, so they continued in silence as Flynn found a spot at the edge of the orange bushes. Valerie's biggest worry was that they would sink into the clay-like ground, so she told Flynn to keep an eye on that and be ready to lift off at the first sign that the *Grandeur* was going down.

"I feel like there's a good joke there," Flynn replied, "but honestly, the massive phallic symbols all over this city make any and all jokes too easy."

Valerie laughed. "I hadn't thought of them in that way."

"You wouldn't." Garcia winked, his eyes flittering to Robin.

"Not sure if I should hit you or merely walk away from that one," Valerie replied, but she couldn't help but smile.

"Hit him," Robin declared. "Definitely hit him."

Valerie opted out of it for now, but said she owed him one and would deliver when he least suspected. Soon they were ready to go, and only Jilla and Flynn stayed back to guard the ship this time.

Faces poked out, then someone emerged, glancing at them before running away.

"Going to get someone to speak with us, I hope," Garcia suggested.

"That, or find a big-ass gun to blow us away with," Robin replied.

Bob guffawed. "Hey, I haven't been blown lately, so if that's as close as I can get—"

"Shut the fuck up, Bob," Valerie interrupted. "If they wanted to blow us away, they would've tried during our descent. And if anyone wanted to blow you, you— Huh, I got nothing."

Garcia laughed. "You looking for an insult there, or..."

"I'm not sure, actually," she admitted. "A joke, but I just kind of blanked."

"Like Flynn said, it's the massive phallic symbols."

"I can't think of them as anything else now," Valerie admitted.

"Back on the topic of being getting blown..." Bob interrupted, glancing at Robin. She hit him hard on the shoulder.

"Ow! I didn't say anything...exactly."

"Your look implied it, and I don't give rainchecks on hitting people," Robin countered.

"Come on, my options are very limited here," Bob argued. "I mean, there are two Earth women—"

"Vampires," Valerie corrected him. "Well, kinda."

"Fine. Two Earth *vampires* here, and that's it. So unless I want to be hooking up with someone who has blue, green, or tattooed skin—maybe orange, I guess—I have to hit on the two of you."

"You'd be barking up the wrong tree," Garcia told him.

"I've dated men," Valerie argued. "But...he's right. Sorry."

Bob glanced at Robin hopefully, and she hit him again.

"Dammit, Robin," he whined, rubbing his arm.

"Hey, I've made my position on this very clear," she replied, then turned to look up at the buildings. "Impressive, though why not build outward instead of up?"

"I don't think they're built," Garcia said, stopping to assess one. "Look here—it's like they grow right out of the ground."

"Weird!" Bob exclaimed.

"Creepy." Robin shuddered.

"They are part of the earth." A female was walking toward them. Sunlight gleamed off her so that at first all they could see was her silhouette. She wasn't a petite female. As she grew closer, it became clear that it wasn't fat or muscle that gave her frame its girth, but carapace. Almost rock, but gleaming—it was somewhere between rock and metal.

"Norrul?" Valerie asked.

The female bowed her head slightly. Now they could see her carapace wasn't like armor, as it had been on other Norrul she had run into—the slaves of the Skulla. This female had metallic rock sticking out of her cheekbones and skull, almost like square horns.

"It depends who's asking," the female replied. "We would ask that you keep our location secret."

"*Escaped* Norrul?" Valerie asked.

Again with the head-bow. "Some of us, yes. Others are here to help those who have escaped; to facilitate it. Which is why I must ask...friend or foe?"

"We have no intention of telling anyone where you are." Valerie answered for the group. "And since you didn't try to attack us, 'friend.'"

The female offered a smile—a weird expression on her face, since it caused her hard skin to wrinkle around the protrusions. "Call me Moralu. You have arrived at an odd time, in that we are celebrating an old religious custom."

"Goodie," Bob exclaimed, glancing around. "A party?"

"Of a sort," Moralu agreed, gesturing to them to follow her. Valerie debated asking about Silahu now, but decided to wait and get a feel for where this female's loyalties really lay. After all, if she were with the enemy, she couldn't have her notifying their leader of Valerie's intentions.

The team followed Moralu as the female explained how they celebrated the planet; how the rocks and metal within gave them life, so they showed it their gratitude. She led them into a larger tower toward the middle, but once inside they went down instead of up. The ramp circled like a spiral staircase, and again seemed to have grown naturally from the clay.

At the bottom of the ramp was a large underground area where many more of these hybrid Norrul had gathered in celebration.

They cheered, some performing an odd dance that involved slamming into one another, others participating in what looked like fight rings—circles of Norruls who watched as three or four went at each other. And at the outskirts of this all, a line of them stood with their hands pressed to the metallic walls, heads bowed as if in prayer.

Nearby Norrul stopped to look at the newcomers.

Some wore frowns, but they backed off at a gesture from Moralu.

"They are not used to outsiders, and this is a very special time," she explained. "But you are my guests. Come, let us talk over here."

She gestured to one of the fighting circles. "These fighters will not hurt the others, or at least nothing that they can't recover from in a few days at most. It's a show of strength and sacrifice, to tell the planet we will defend her."

Two of the Norrul turned on third, grabbing his carapace and heaving him against the wall, where a fourth commenced beating on him.

"Seems very...respectful," Bob remarked, frowning and ignoring the look Valerie shot his way to get him to shut up.

"We all have our own strange customs," Moralu said. "I hear that on Earth they cut out hearts and eat them? Those of your own people, and slaves."

"A long time ago," Bob countered.

"Is that so?" She shrugged. "My information is what it is, and 'long' is relative term."

"It is," Valerie agreed, trying to change the subject.

"What brings you to us?" Moralu asked.

Valerie hesitated, but no good excuses came. "Have you heard of the corporation called 'Silahu?'"

Moralu's change in expression was barely noticeable, but was there nonetheless. "Why do you ask?"

"We assumed they were a large part of the economy here," Garcia interjected. "Is that the case?"

"They are."

"We're looking for their headquarters," Valerie told

Moralu, although she hated to give up this information. "Any chance you can point us in the right direction?"

"They come through from time to time, flying their goods to and fro in the galaxy. Maybe beyond." Moralu shrugged. "I've never been there, but I can tell you the direction in which their ships have flown."

"Thank you," Valerie replied. "We would appreciate that."

"But of course."

"After they join us," a male declared, stepping up behind Moralu. His carapace was like hers, only more metallic than stone, and spiked. "Show us you can be trusted."

"Rokal," Moralu said, again displaying that hesitant look in her eyes. "They have nothing to prove to you."

He didn't even look her way. His eyes were focused on Valerie. "It's not about proving anything, simply joining us in the celebration."

"You don't have to do this," Moralu cautioned.

"Oh, but I'd love to." Valerie removed her helmet and handed it to Robin, then stepped out of her armor so that she only wore her black and red uniform. " I've never backed away from a fight, friendly," she maintained eye contact with the male, "or otherwise."

"Wonderful!" Rokal exclaimed, and a slight smile appeared on Moralu's face. Had she wanted this too? Or maybe she really wanted Rokal to get his ass kicked, and now was the time.

"I don't know if it's smart to show up and humiliate them right away," Robin remarked, partly to Valerie, but also as a jab at the male.

Valerie simply smiled politely as she rotated her arms to loosen up her shoulders. "Point me to it."

"Think I don't know who you are?" Rokal asked as he moved others aside so that they could enter the circle, from which two Norruls were dragging a third.

"I'm intrigued to find out how and why you would," she shot back.

"Maybe you've made on impression on others of our kind," he offered. "Maybe they've spread word to our higher-ups to be on the lookout for you. And after the way you handled Tol and the Damu Michezo, you can be sure you've gotten their attention."

"Are we talking those who have a problem with what I did there?"

The metallic horns shifted as his expression changed to one that resembled annoyance. "They might not care, but the follow-up situation has them greatly vexed."

"Sslake?" she asked.

He nodded. "Everyone thought he was dead."

Others were cheering now as two more Norrul stepped into the circle, and Valerie had to speak up to be heard.

"And he's not. Where does that leave us with your friends?"

He held out his hands. "They'd like to meet you. They think you're very powerful; an ally we would be glad to have on our side. But I'm skeptical. All I see before me is a puny female without a shell. Prove me wrong."

"I don't have to prove shit to anyone," she replied, "but I'll gladly help celebrate, if this is the way to do so."

"Indeed." He turned to the crowd. "An Earther from the Pan galaxy!"

A mix of cheering and confused murmurs followed.

"She wishes to show her respect for our ways," Moralu chimed in. "So show her *your* respect."

Now the crowd cheered, though it was clearly half-hearted.

The other two Norruls had already started moving around the circle, getting a feel for Rokal and Valerie, but Rokal didn't seem impressed. He was still playing to the crowd to work their excitement up, and roared at one of the other Norrul in the circle with him.

In a rush, both the Norruls charged him. He moved fast though, seemingly lighter on his feet than his opponents, and maneuvered to sweep one's legs and toss him straight at Valerie. When had she ever not been ready? With a backwards roll she tossed him up and over, and then—oh, damn—got her answer. She wasn't ready for Rokal's ax-kick. It caught her in the sternum before she had made it up, and sent her right back down.

The blow was like a steel battering ram. For a moment she lay there catching her breath, but the next blow came and she had to get out of the way. As she rolled, the other Norrul caught her by the hair and pulled her up.

This wasn't going nearly as well as she'd expected it to.

Rokal came in like she was a punching bag, and Valerie was vaguely aware of Robin screaming for her to keep her arms up and defend herself. An old hatred—her hatred of pain—revived itself as those metal-covered limbs came at her, his fists slamming into her like cars.

For a while she'd gotten used to pain. It was nothing but an inconvenience. But she'd hated it, and avoided it at all costs. At that moment she remembered why.

It fucking *hurt*!

She wasn't going to take any more of this. When the next blow came, she pulled back and wrapped an arm around the one holding her, sucking up the pain that came from the top of her head as he restrained her by the hair. Her other arm took Rokal's blow and then wrapped around his arm, and she used her enhanced strength to slam Rokal into the weaker Norrul.

Considering the strength she had put into that blow, she was surprised either still stood. Rokal stumbled back, blood all over his front, but when he looked up she could see it wasn't his. The other Norrul had taken those horns to the skull, and was on his knees, wailing. Others came in to take him to be cared for. The other Norrul charged at her, shouting, but Valerie was past the point of giving a shit if she hurt them. No more pain…for her.

Pushing off the ground, she kicked out at her new opponent with both legs, then followed up with a one-two punch to his neck. He gagged and fell back into the crowd. Meanwhile, Rokal had clearly recovered. The proof was the strike that caught Valerie in the back, followed by a punch to the kidneys that would've had her pissing blood for a month if she didn't have the ability to heal.

She turned on him with a growl. Her eyes glowed and her fangs were extended, and she grabbed him by the metal horns sticking out of his head. He didn't seem worried about that…not until she dropped to one knee and took him down with her, slamming his face into the ground. When she pulled the horns in separate directions, metal scraping on bone by the sound of it, he started screaming.

Blood seeped around one of the horns, and she pulled

until skin ripped. Then Moralu was there, pulling her back and shouting that it was enough.

Rokal glanced up with anger in his eyes and she prepared to take the fight to the next level, but he collapsed, growling but submitting.

"Winner!" Moralu announced, gesturing to Valerie. A moment of silence followed, during which Valerie thought they'd string her up and tear her to pieces. Cheering ensued instead, and the celebration continued.

"What's wrong with you all?" Robin asked Moralu, stepping over to check on Valerie.

"Pain, violence…" Moralu licked her lips. "It's part of our lives and our culture. If we can learn to embrace it, nothing can faze us."

"Which," Rokal said in a trembling voice as he managed to get to his feet behind them, "is why you might think you pissed me off, but actually you've just earned my respect and taught me a very valuable lesson."

"Not to get your ass handed to you?" Robin asked. Valerie shot her a "shut up" glance.

"Actually, yes," Rokal admitted, smiling. Blood crept down his forehead in a line, then dripped from the ridge of his brow.

"Now, you were asking about the Silahu Corporation?" He grinned. "Let me get cleaned up, and I'll show you the way."

"You'd do that?" Valerie asked.

"I'd say it's a trap," Robin offered. "After the way you just demolished him?"

He looked offended by her remark. "We are Norrul. You showed your strength, and to us that's all that matters. I wasn't humiliated out there. I was bested, and shown a vision of greatness."

Valerie laughed. "Keep kissing my ass and we'll be good friends in no time."

He frowned. "I'm sorry, but... I don't really find you attractive, nor would I ever—"

"Ah, translation issue," Valerie interrupted, holding up her hands. "Sorry, it means, like... Huh, 'laying it on thick?' Complimenting too much when you don't have to."

"Earthers use a phrase that means putting your lips on someone's poop hole to convey that?" Moralu asked, her frown as severe as the look of disgust on Rokal's face.

Garcia had joined them, and now laughed. "You have no idea how nasty some Earthers can get, believe me. I mean, not that I do, but... Trust me."

"Let's not share those kinds of details," Valerie said, face-palming. "Can we just... Rokal, was it? Get cleaned up, and then yes, please. Show us."

"And there will be no lips on poop holes, we promise," Robin told them with a chuckle, earning her a fist-bump from Garcia.

"You all are strange," Moralu stated, watching Rokal stumble off. "Now, about that one..."

"Yes?" Valerie asked.

"I'm not sure how far you can trust him. Just...be wary, yes?"

"Would you be willing to show us the way instead?" Valerie asked.

Moralu's eyes narrowed. "As I earlier stated, I can point you in the right direction."

"Then we'll go with the guide we can get."

"What's so important that you have to deal with them?"

"A weapons deal," Valerie answered.

It was clear Moralu didn't buy that. "Don't get your hopes up."

Valerie nodded as Rokal returned in armor and helmet, with a rifle slung over his shoulder.

"You have your own ship?" Valerie asked.

"What sort of guide would I be without one?" he responded, and grinned. His horns were still bent awkwardly but had been wrapped and taped, although blood was already seeping through the bandages.

"Sorry about that," Valerie said, gesturing at his horns.

He grinned. "Makes me look unique. The ladies will love it."

"That true?" Robin asked Moralu.

The two Norruls exchanged a glare, then Rokal headed for the door. "You coming?"

Valerie waved the rest of her group on, since she'd noticed the look of concern Moralu gave her. She wanted to tell the female not to worry, but she herself was curious about what might happen. Maybe there *was* reason to worry? Either way, the mission had to continue.

CHAPTER SEVEN

SWARTHIAN EXTENDED DETENTION ENVIRONMENT (SEDE)

Kalan went through the door and followed the Wearl's voice out of the garbage room into a low hallway. He had to crouch so low he was nearly on his knees as he walked.

"Sorry it took me so long," she whispered. "I considered going after Nostro and forcing him to let you out, but his place is even better protected than Captain Tuttle's chambers."

"So how'd you do it?"

"I had a little help. I'm taking you to her now. We're about to get into a more populated area, so we need to be quiet."

They exited the low passage a few moments later and came out on an empty walkway. Kalan stayed low, hoping not to be spotted.

Wearl made soft clicking noises—with her tongue,

Kalan presumed—so that he could follow her. Thankfully it wasn't a long walk.

They reached a dark doorway toward the end of the walkway and Wearl whispered, "Get inside."

Kalan did as she asked.

An elderly Pallicon female was seated at a table just inside the room. She wore a scowl, but she looked entirely unsurprised to find a large gray rock of a male entering her home.

"Don't *you* smell nice," she said dryly.

"Yes, sorry about that, ma'am. I was in the—"

"I know, I know—the garbage pit. How do you think your friend got in there? Everything go all right, Wearl?"

"Exactly like you said it would," the Shimmer replied. "Kalan, meet Hattor."

"Pleased to meet you, ma'am."

The elderly Pallicon looked him up and down. "I thought you said he was cute, Wearl."

"He is." Wearl sounded shocked that anyone could possibly think otherwise.

Hattor sighed. "I must be out of my mind, letting in a stranger who pissed off Nostro. Wearl as much as admitted you're here on a mission from Captain Tuttle to drag Nostro out of here. What do you think he'll do to me if he learns I helped you?"

Kalan pulled out one of the chairs in front of the table and squeezed himself into it. "Maybe we can help. We've seen how everyone is so afraid of him. We're here to take him down. The One-Eight-Nine doesn't have to live in fear."

Hattor chuckled softly. "I think you may have the wrong idea about this place."

"How so?"

"The guards are afraid of Nostro, yes, but everyone else? Not so much."

Kalan raised an eyebrow. "What do you mean?"

She thought a moment. "Let me tell you a story. Nostro was born in SEDE, just like you. Though a decade or so before you, if I had to guess. By the time he was fifteen, he had the respect of everyone on the cellblock."

Kalan grimaced. "I guess some kingpins start early."

Hattor shook her head. "It wasn't like that. He wasn't trying to control his fellow prisoners. He was trying to help them. They would come to him with problems. Whether it was another prisoner stealing from them or harassing them, or it was a guard mistreating them, Nostro was unafraid. He'd do anything to help them."

"Good way to get his hooks in them," Wearl observed. "Get everyone to owe you a favor or two, then when everyone owes you something, you take control."

Hattor shook her head again. "You still don't understand. He never asked for anything in return. He only wanted to help. To make things fair for those who weren't strong enough to fight for themselves."

"Hmm," Kalan mused. "It almost sounds like you're describing a hero."

Hattor shrugged. "Call it what you will. All I know is he helped a lot of people."

"So what happened?"

"The same thing that happens to every sabie. He turned eighteen. When he aged out of SEDE, we gave him a send-off like the One-Eight-Nine had never seen. Sometimes when young 'uns leave, you get a feeling they'll be back here. Other ones, you're not so sure. It's tough to make it on the outside when you grew up here. As you well know."

Kalan acknowledged that with a nod. In truth, it wasn't that difficult to make a life; what was difficult was making a life on the right side of the law. That was why so many sabies ended up back in SEDE within a year or two.

Hattor continued, "With Nostro, I was certain. I knew I'd never see him again. He'd have a future in the military. Or government. Or maybe command his own ship. That one could do anything he put his mind to, and I knew he'd put his mind to great things. Imagine my disappointment when he showed up back at SEDE three months later."

"What happened?" Wearl asked.

Hattor shook her head. "He wouldn't say, but there were rumors. Some said he purposely got caught committing a crime. That he wanted to come back."

It was a story Kalan had heard before with other sabies. "He couldn't handle life on the outside?"

"No, it wasn't that. More like he couldn't handle thinking of his friends and family living in the One-Eight-Nine without him there to help them. All I know for sure is that things were different when he got back inside. The guards had always dealt with him slightly differently than everyone else—like they respected him. But when he got back, the guards started to fear him. They started doing whatever he wanted. He even made them reprogram our translation chips so we could hear their voices."

"And you have no idea how he did it?"

"Nope. The only thing I can think of is that something

happened on the outside that totally changed his status for them. Most of the Shimmer guards seem to truly love and respect him."

"He's like the anti-Kalan then," Wearl joked.

Hattor paused for a moment. "I think it's time for you to meet Nostro for real. To have a conversation with him."

"He didn't like us much the last time," Kalan pointed out.

"True, but you had been sent to drag him out of his home, so you can't really blame him."

Kalan had to admit she had a point there.

"I believe you two have good hearts. We just have to get Nostro to listen to you long enough for him to see that for himself."

"And how are you going to get him to do that?" Wearl asked.

Hattor smiled. "He has to listen to me. I'm his mother."

Kalan's mouth dropped open. "Why didn't you tell us earlier?"

"Where's the fun in that?" She stood up slowly from the table. "Come on, let's go see my son. I'll make sure he doesn't throw you in the garbage this time."

Kalan stood and followed her to the door. "That would be greatly appreciated."

The Pallicon led them out of her home and down the walkway, but then she surprised Kalan by taking a left turn into what should have been a dead end—only in One-Eight-Nine, it wasn't. It led to a tunnel that appeared to run behind the prisoners' quarters.

"You'll want to watch your step," Hattor told them as they entered the tunnel. "Nostro had this place built after he returned. He wanted to be able to come and go without being seen."

"Why's that?" Kalan asked.

"He leaves the cellblock sometimes. He won't tell me where he goes, but I have the feeling he's investigating something."

"If he's going to do that, he should—" Wearl's words cut off mid-sentence, replaced by a surprised shout. The ground beneath her gave way and she started to fall.

Kalan flung his arm out, grabbing blindly. His fingers closed around her wrist and he pulled her back up.

Hattor laughed and called, "Sorry, my fault. I should have mentioned that he's got some booby traps in here. Doesn't want his enemies using it to sneak up on him."

"Like we're doing?" Kalan asked.

"Exactly. Just stay to the center of the walkway and you'll be fine."

They made their way in silence for a few minutes before Hattor stopped in front of what appeared to be a dead end.

"When I open this door, we'll be in his quarters. Stay quiet, and let me do the talking. He can be a bit of a hothead at times. Once I've explained, you can have a conversation with him.

With that, she touched a spot on the tunnel wall and a panel slid open, revealing a numbered keypad. Hattor entered a ten-digit number and a door opened.

They went through into a dark room. Once Kalan's eyes adjusted, he nearly gasped. They weren't just in Nostro's quarters; they were in his bedroom. The Pallicon leader was sleeping in his bed right in front of them.

For a brief moment it crossed Kalan's mind how easy it would be to subdue the old Pallicon female, grab Nostro, and head back to the captain.

But no. She had trusted them. He owed her the respect of hearing her out.

Hattor took a step toward her son's bed, but he spoke before she reached him.

"Kalan Grayhewn."

All three of the intruders froze in surprise.

"You know, there's a reason we throw our enemies in the garbage pit," Nostro continued. "It's not just to be jerks. We want it to be impossible for you to sneak up on us if and when you get out. You smell like absolute trash... which is the whole point. I would like to know how you got out, though."

"Um, yeah, interesting story about that," Kalan said. "I actually had help from—"

Nostro suddenly rolled over, leaping from his bed, a metal bar in his hand. His eyes found Kalan and he lunged at him.

Kalan barely deflected the blow, taking in on the arm instead of in the face. He grunted in pain as his arm went numb.

"Nostro, stop," Hattor commanded.

The big Pallicon froze, shocked at the unexpected voice. "Mom?"

"Of course it's Mom. Who else has the code to your secret entrance?"

Nostro shuffled to the wall and clicked a switch. The room filled with warm light, and Nostro looked at them in confusion.

For the first time, Kalan saw Nostro's face. It was absolutely hideous, covered with weird growths, strange hair-like tentacles, and two flaring holes where the nostrils should have been. He wondered why in the world a Pallicon who could look like anything he wanted would choose to look like that.

"These two *were* sent by the captain, just as you thought," Hattor told him.

"Two? Oh, the Shimmer must be here as well."

"You're damn right I am," Wearl said.

Hattor continued, "But they're out to do the right thing. They thought you were abusing the prisoners of the One-Eight-Nine."

"Of course that's what the captain would tell them." He paused for a moment. "I had my Shimmers fill me in on some of your exploits while you were in the pit. That was why I put you there—to give me time to find the truth."

"Yeah?" Kalan asked. "What did you find out?"

"Enough to make me trust you, at least temporarily. I don't think you would be working for Captain Tuttle if you knew the truth. There's too much information on the people you've helped, starting with Sslake."

Kalan thought for a moment. He was impressed by how quickly Nostro had changed his mind about them once he knew the truth, but he wasn't ready to let the garbage pit episode go that easily. "And what about you? Why should we trust you?"

Nostro chuckled. "I guess I'll have to prove myself."

"Maybe you could start by telling us the truth. Why'd you come back to SEDE?"

"To help my fellow prisoners," he responded immediately.

"That's pretty vague. I need specifics. How were you planning to help them?"

Nostro paused for a moment, as if considering whether to answer that question. "By taking down Tuttle."

The answer surprised Kalan a little. "Tuttle stays out of our cellblocks. Stays out of the prisoners' lives for the most part. You really think he's the problem here?"

Nostro nodded. "Tuttle isn't here for any sort of rehabilitation of the prisoners. He's working toward a secret purpose. I haven't figured it all out yet, but he's actually working for this being called 'High Priest Demustrius.' The guy is obsessed with justice, only I'm not totally sure he even knows what that word means. He seems to think the only way for the galaxy to be just is for him to control it."

That did sound a bit familiar. Captain Tuttle had talked a lot about justice when he'd given Kalan and Wearl the job.

Nostro took a step toward Kalan. "You know Sslake, right?"

Kalan nodded. "I haven't talked to him in a while, but I did rescue him from SEDE, so I think he'd take my call."

"And I was his cellmate," Wearl interjected.

"Excellent," Nostro exclaimed. "If I can get you proof of what Tuttle's up to and I help you escape, will you tell Sslake what's really going on here? He has the power to fire Captain Tuttle."

A smile crept across Kalan's face. "You want to help us escape, and all we have to do is have a conversation with Sslake? Yeah, I think that will work just fine."

Nostro smiled back, and the movement made his facial tentacles wiggle strangely. "No time like the present. Let's get started."

Hattor put a hand on her son's arm. "I knew you kids would get along. Have fun with your escape attempt."

"Thanks, Mom." Nostro gave her a kiss on the head, then turned to Kalan. "Right. Let's get started."

CHAPTER EIGHT

PLANET RHOL, SILAHU COMPOUND

The *Grandeur* approached Silahu compound cautiously, everyone aboard aware that there could be all sorts of defensive mechanisms in place. Rokal's one-person ship led the way, so far without incident.

"No missile lock, no sign of anti-aircraft," Flynn reported, checking the display.

"Incoming aircraft?" Valerie asked, totally confused why she hadn't seen any yet. "I know you're good at flying under the radar, but *that* good?"

"I got us in against Aranaught," he countered.

"And we'll forever sing your praises for it," Garcia interjected. "But right now, this isn't making sense. Where the hell are they?"

Jilla cleared her throat. "I've heard stories, from years ago."

"What kind of stories?" Valerie asked.

"About the cruelty of the corporation here—Silahu. They were the type of place you didn't mess with."

"Meaning?"

"If they haven't attacked us yet, something's up," she explained. "Maybe an ambush, or—"

"Or that," Flynn interrupted, pointing at the display. On the screen was a magnified view of one particular area of the planet below—a large compound in ruins.

"Silahu," Jilla said, pointing to a sign with alien script that was still readable. "What happened here?"

All were silent as they approached, soon able to see the devastation without the on-screen enhancement. The earth around the compound was scorched. Walls still stood in places, as well as two of the buildings, but mostly it had been destroyed.

There were crashed ships scattered about as well, and one still had smoke coming from it.

"Holy shit," Bob exclaimed, "this was recent."

Valerie gulped. "Flynn, check for enemy activity nearby. Not on planet, but above."

He did so, but shook his head. "I'm not showing anyone out there. Whatever did this is either long gone, or was destroyed along with the rest."

"Well, we have to get down there and see if anyone's still alive," she pointed out.

As Flynn began the descent, he added, "And if so, were they designers."

"Right, and that."

A message came up on the display, and when Flynn brought it up they saw Rokal's ugly face staring at them.

"Are you seeing this?" he asked. "Not exactly what we were expecting."

"Not at all," Valerie conceded. "You didn't know anything about an attack?"

"Negative. Come to think of it, an hour or so earlier and we might've been involved. Good thing we're late to the party!"

"I wouldn't call it a party," Valerie replied, unable to take her eyes off the wreckage. "We're going down."

"Me too, then. I'll see you there."

They approached the ruins, continuing to scan but coming up with nothing. When they landed, Valerie insisted everyone suit up in full-body armor and helmets. She had everyone but Robin stay back to guard the ship and be ready to take off, in case there were problems.

"And you two?" Garcia asked.

Robin snickered. "What, you don't think we can handle ourselves?"

"The rest of us can't?"

She shrugged and let Valerie handle it.

"While you're enhanced, and I get that, the point remains that Robin and I can move faster and heal from worse injuries."

"You don't think we'd benefit by having a second team out there searching?" Jilla asked.

"We might," Valerie conceded. "I'll want people watching my back in case Rokal tries something. Flynn, I want you ready to fly the ship out of here if necessary, and we'll want an extra guard. "Garcia and Bob, then? You two head left and search for ways in."

"What exactly are we looking for?" Bob asked.

"A map of sorts, we think," Valerie answered. "A way to activate the base. Information on some defensible planet, or whatever it is Admiral Lolack believes is out here."

"For what it's worth, that's a false story," Jilla told them. "I've heard it, but I don't believe it."

"Like an urban legend?" Robin asked.

"That doesn't translate. Not a legend, though—just a story that everyone shares, but isn't real. At least, there's no proof of it."

"There's no proof as far as you are concerned that a vampire named Michael walked our Earth, could talk in people's minds, take the form of mist—kinda—and basically shoot lightning."

Jilla started laughing. "Your point? Of course there's not. How could... Oh, shit, you're serious?"

"Deadly serious." Robin grinned.

"Okay, I don't believe that either." Jilla frowned. "Another urban legend."

"He was real," Valerie said. "Gave me the ability to do this." She felt her anger rise at the idea of someone questioning Michael's existence, and it helped with the effect as her eyes turned red and her fangs extended.

She'd been able to do some pretty badass shit back on Earth, such as *pushing* fear onto her enemies so that they'd more or less piss themselves. Up here, though, it had different effects, based on the alien race she used it on. Based on what it had done to the healing Pallicons back on Tol when she'd taken down their fighting system, *pushing* fear on Jilla's type made them unable to heal or transform. That was a little fact she could save for later, though.

"We've wasted enough time," Robin pointed out, nodding at the door.

Jilla stared, open-mouthed, then blinked. "So it's true. Damn, Kalan told me about you, but I just figured—"

"That it was more lies?" Valerie laughed, letting her eyes and teeth return to normal. "There are worse monsters in this universe than us, I imagine. But not many."

"In that case, I'm glad to be on your side." Jilla transformed to look like Valerie had a moment ago, eyes red and fangs extending. "But it still could be lies."

Valerie smiled and *pushed* fear—and smiled wider when Jilla tried to transform back, but couldn't.

"Whatever you're doing to me, it's not funny," Jilla said, red eyes darting around the room. "Please stop."

Valerie did, then nodded. "Just so we're clear. No lies from me—ever."

"Got it."

Valerie glanced at Robin, who was at the door and gesturing for her to leave. The woman's narrowed eyes were visible through the helmet's faceplate. Showing off might not have been necessary...but then again, it was important to have the respect of everyone on the team. Jilla had asked for it.

They exited, finding Rokal already starting to work his way through the debris. He wore his armor and helmet, and had his rifle at the ready.

"So, no weapons deal," he said.

Valerie could tell by the tone of his voice that he hadn't expected this to be about a weapons deal. Still, she replied, "That's too bad. Maybe they had the shipment ready, and we can still find it."

He gestured toward one of the partially destroyed buildings. "That's our best bet."

She nodded and followed him in that direction.

"When do we tell him what we're really after?" Robin asked.

"When it's the only way we'll find it," Valerie replied. "I'd just as soon have him gone. There's something about him..."

"Aside from the fact that he tried to tear you to pieces back there?"

"Who hasn't?" Valerie scanned the area for any signs of a way down, or what might be the main part of their headquarters. "Hell, when we met you were a trained vampire assassin, right? You would've killed me if given the chance."

"Only if forced," Robin countered. "Though I've been tempted sometimes since then."

"Shut up! You have not."

Robin shrugged.

"When?" Valerie demanded. "When have I been such a pain that you wanted to kill me?"

"Fine, not actually *kill* you. But you've been a pain."

Valerie frowned, stopping the search to look at her friend. "Name one time."

"Seriously, you don't know?" Robin laughed, but kept moving. "How about not so long ago when you started flirting with me again out of the blue."

"I wasn't flirting with you."

Robin glanced at her and laughed.

"Okay, maybe," Valerie admitted. "That annoyed you so much?" She jogged to catch up with the woman. "No, answer me! My feelings for you annoyed you to the point that you'd say you wanted to kill me?"

"I shouldn't have used those words," Robin agreed, but turned back to Valerie and finally stopped. "Listen, it's not just that you have feelings for me. It's that I have feelings for you, too."

"What?" That stunned Valerie, causing her to feel like she'd just been shoved.

"Of course I do!" Robin turned as if to keep walking, but then looked back at Valerie. " I can't focus out here while looking at your lips every five seconds and wondering when they'll touch mine again, or...or... Shut up. You get the picture."

Now Robin did walk off, heading toward Rokal. She left Valerie staring after her with a new realization taking hold. If this ended—if they could beat this force coming at them—maybe that would be enough for this part of the universe? Set things straight in this galaxy by dealing with multiple enemies from multiple galaxies, and talk about allies for the Etheric Federation.

Maybe if that happened, they'd be able to take a breather. Relax, maybe take a vacation.

Not feel distracted by their feelings, but rather be allowed to pursue them. More than ever, Valerie felt the urge to complete this mission. She jogged past them, eyes searching.

In one of the building remnants, they found an old holographic display that played music and walked visitors through a history of the corporation. It even hit on making the economy better for the locals, but was ultimately a waste of time.

Valerie spoke into her comm. "Any news?"

"All clear here," Garcia replied.

"Nothing happening on the ship," Flynn reported.

Valerie shared a frustrated look with Robin, but pushed on. Soon they had found another building fragment, though it was only a few rooms. One of them, however, had a walkway down, partially blocked by fallen rubble.

The two worked to move the rubble aside, then got the jammed door open.

"What've we got?" Rokal asked from their left.

"Maybe nothing," Valerie said, glancing around. She wasn't sure if she'd expected to find an army of Norrul waiting to ambush them or what, but it seemed clear.

Some of the rubble moved...then silence.

Valerie stepped toward the sound, cocking her head. "Whoever's there, come out nice and slow."

When nothing happened, Robin said, "Could be an animal."

"Or shifts in the ground," Rokal added.

"It's not," Valerie replied, when one of her other powers kicked in. She'd been able to sense the emotions of others back on Earth. It was almost like reading minds, as more powerful vampires could do, but her version was more like a generic sense of their emotions. It often played out as warmth or cold, sometimes clear, sometimes not.

Here it was coming at her like radar. Just as the fear power worked differently on other races, this did too, apparently—only that sense had been silent until now. Suddenly it was sending her throbbing pulses, coming from the direction where she'd seen movement.

"Back up," she hissed at Robin, raising her rifle.

Again the rubble moved, and this time a hand emerged. It pushed out farther, scattering the pieces of cement and metal, then another hand.

"What do we do?" Robin asked.

"Might be friendly," Valerie answered. "Won't find out unless we ask."

"Dammit!" Robin exclaimed, but nodded. "I'll cover you, in case."

Valerie stepped forward, letting her rifle drop on its sling. If the situation got out of control she could handle herself with just her hands, but right now she didn't want to appear threatening.

"I'm going to help you," she said as she knelt to grab one of the hands. In a quick jerk she had the figure out of the rubble, then lowered him to sit. Judging by the body armor and face behind that faceplate it was a he, but he looked strange—scaly skin, green and purple, like eggplant meets lizard. His eyes were white slits with no visible pupils. Unlike their faceplates his opened to the sides, rising in a V shape.

"Were you with the company?" she asked.

His nose slits closed and opened again, then he said, "Yes. Silahu."

"Can you tell us what happened here?"

"Not...much. I remember an attack. I ran to get my gear, as was standard practice in case...and I made it."

Valerie glanced back at Robin, who shrugged. They didn't know if they could trust this guy, but they needed to find out if he knew anything, so she'd play along but be ready.

"Can you show us where you worked?" Valerie asked.

He glanced around, playing it very well if he was an enemy. Either way he was dazed, unsure about his next move.

Then he saw Rokal approaching, and his eyes went wide. "No!"

Valerie spun, but it was too late—Rokal already had his rifle out, finger on the trigger. With a burst of shots, the stranger fell to the ground, blood spurting from his head and neck. Neither Valerie nor Robin responded since Rokal's action had been such a shock, until the Norrul was on the stranger, pounding his face in with the rifle. Something rolled out of the stranger's hand and Rokal was on it, snatching it up and running at the same time.

"The *fuck*?" Robin asked.

"We heard shooting," Garcia said over the comm, snapping Valerie out of it. She was about to go after Rokal, to toss him to the ground and beat the answers out of him to all the questions spinning around in her head at that moment, when shots pounded the ground between them and the Norrul. Large shots—enough to make small craters.

She pulled back, shielding herself from the flying debris, and glanced at the stranger to confirm he was indeed dead. Face smashed in, head now convex. Yup, definitely deceased.

"I think we've been had," Robin said, pointing up.

"You all seeing this?" Garcia's voice came through again.

Valerie followed Robin's gesture and saw a series if ships above them, some out of atmosphere, some in.

She swore. "The Norrul back there—or maybe just Rokal, if he was working alone—notified the enemy."

"What do we do here?" Flynn asked over the comm.

"Stand by," Valerie ordered, noting that just one medium-sized ship was approaching. "See if you can contact Lolack, or actually Tenowk."

"Roger that."

The descending ship had to be about twice the size of the *Grandeur*, but more angular. It looked like blown glass in a thunderstorm. It was red with gold trim, matching one of the other, much larger ships above.

"A transport ship for someone rather important, I'm guessing," Valerie said.

"Looks about right," Robin replied, glancing at the body again. "Guessing here... Rokal had been part of the attack on these people here, maybe known this guy at the time, but thought he'd gotten away. Was back with the Norrul, figured he could lead us out here to be captured when we found this guy."

"Sure, except..." Valerie gestured toward Rokal's ship, which was now hightailing it out of there. "Why not bring it to his boss?"

Robin's frown was visible through her faceplate. "Good question."

"I'm thinking our friend Moralu was behind the call. Neither is on our side, but they serve different bosses?"

"Damn. That makes this whole situation that much more complicated."

Valerie nodded, then spoke into her comm. "Flynn, put a tracker on Rokal's ship if possible."

"Tenowk's in the area," Flynn replied. "Well, not really in the *area*, but within reach. He says he was keeping the connection with us alive as long as he could, and that

Lolack's fleet has spotted this other fleet through their systems. They're outnumbered, it appears, but can make a move if necessary."

"Let's hope not," Valerie said, then stopped talking. The ship had landed and the ramp was opening.

Out stepped the most outlandish character she had ever seen. On its head was a grand helmet that was the same chaotic shape as its transport ship. Its body was mostly covered by a green robe, which seemed to be covering armor that had all manner of cables running out of it and behind it to the robotic creatures following it. They were tall and gray, reminding Valerie of Kalan and her desire to find him. The difference was that these creatures had glowing red eyes. She could finally see why that freaked out her enemies when she did it. They also had spiked limbs, and clearly visible projectile weapons.

When the main figure stopped, its voice seemed to echo from all around them as it began, "The one and only Valerie, I presume?"

She was taken aback by the fact that it knew her name, but merely replied, "Yes."

"I've heard such great things," it said, and for a moment it was like a mist of green fogged its helmet, and she was able to see within—as if the fogging worked the opposite way. It was a male, similar to the Norrul, but his protrusions looked to be full metal and connected to his suit.

"And whom do I have the pleasure of addressing?" she said in her most formal tone.

"You may call me Demus, but to all others I am High Priest Demustrius." He stopped moving and his robots formed a semicircle around him, facing her.

"And what have you heard?" Valerie asked.

"Only that you, too, seek justice. That you fight for this justice, and are ruthless in its quest. That you have done great things in the name of justice, as have I." He held out first his right hand, then his left, gesturing to the planet they were on and the universe beyond. "Many planets in the galaxies nearby have agreed. They bow the knee and recognize me as their god to avoid continued injustice. The suffering must stop. The pain must cease. We can make that happen across the rest of the universe."

"'We?'"

"You and I, child," he said, holding a hand out to her now. It was gloved, but seemed warm and inviting.

She resisted the urge to grasp it. "Sir, I assume you've come at the call of the AI, Aranaught."

"She alerted me to a need," he replied cautiously.

"A need to fight Admiral Lolack and his fleet? My friends?"

His hand withdrew. "You would ally yourselves with them? Do you know what evil they've brought upon my kind?"

"Tell me," she requested.

After an audible breath his helmet turned to her and Robin, assessing each of them in turn. "The fleet has stood in my way for too long. If not for them, I would have had my justice long ago. My people would be free, and—"

"The Norrul?" Valerie asked. "That's what this is about? That not all of them are free?"

"In a sense."

"And if they *were* free, you would let the other planets and galaxies be?"

He snorted. "Of course not! No independent planet can be trusted. It is only when you have them under control that you can monitor them, ensure they are playing by the rules." Again he stuck out his hand, more forcibly this time. "For the last time, I give you the option to join me!"

"You'd free your people and claim justice by enslaving everyone else," she asked, unable to hide her disdain. "I don't see any honor or justice in that, only cowardice. Only a megalomaniac who isn't afraid to hurt anyone in his path would do something like that."

The robots around him hissed and took offensive stances, but Demus stood tall, hand still outstretched.

"A firm no, then?" he confirmed.

"That's right."

"Then that's how it is, and this is how it ends for you," he replied, and she heard whirring and electricity formed around his outstretched hand.

"Oh, shit," Robin said, already charging to pull Valerie out of the way. The bolt of lightning that passed them slashed the ground, sending the previous debris flying.

"Everyone on the ship," Valerie shouted into her comm, already up and running with Robin at her side.

"Couldn't we have just shot him in the face?" Robin asked as they leaped over a wall. As soon as they were clear, it exploded in a blast of lightning.

"Something tells me he was ready for that," Valerie countered.

"Still, even just a small slap would've made me feel better."

Valerie chuckled. "From where we are now? Me too!"

Flynn was already in the air and flying toward them, and suddenly swerved as a shot hit right in front of him.

"Where's Garcia?" Valerie asked, glancing around.

"Over here!" came his response, and she saw the two of them almost at the ship, near where the shot had hit. The ramp had opened and they had just entered when another bolt flashed. This one hit the *Grandeur*, apparently taking a chunk out of shields and sending the ship off-course.

"Behind the building," Valerie shouted into her comm, and she and Robin changed course to their left.

"They're shooting from above," Robin pointed out.

"At least he won't be able to see *us* to shoot that lightning," Valerie replied, gesturing to the way the ground sunk down behind the nearest cliff face. Still, Robin had a point and the shots from above kept raining down.

A shot came close enough to cause Valerie to have to leap sideways when she noticed the shadow, the next striking the ground between her and Robin. A horrific moment passed when Valerie thought her friend had been hit, but Robin came charging through the smoke and grabbed her by the forearm, and the two were on their way again.

"On the other side," Valerie told Flynn, and watched as the ship disappeared. "We're coming from the roof."

"What?" Robin asked doubtfully.

"So they don't expect it," Valerie answered.

They reached the edge of the building and Valerie led the way, using the back fence to leap up and onto the roof. They scrambled to their feet to jump to the next one as a blast of lightning hit nearby and the roof burst into flames.

"You've got to be kidding me!" Robin exclaimed, then shouted, "This was your plan?"

"Keep up, slow poke," Valerie replied, and reached the highest point. "Now, Flynn!"

The *Grandeur* appeared, ascending with ramp down and pointed their direction. Valerie pulled Robin up and they ran and leaped for the ramp, landing as the ship started to pull away.

"Get us out of here!" Garcia shouted, pulling them in. "We've got them."

"Tenowk!" Flynn called, and there was a shout of frustration from Demus, followed by a response that sounded like the IAI's voice.

"I blocked them momentarily, but it won't hold long. There's something about these guys; some force pushing back, like a counterbalance to Aranaught."

"Not quite their own AI," Aranaught's voice came through, "but something just as powerful, or more so."

"Do we have a trace on Rokal and whatever he grabbed?" Valerie asked as the ramp closed. She was damn glad to have made it.

"Thanks to Tenowk," Flynn said, turning with a smile to see her. They saw only sky and space ahead as they quickly left the planet behind.

"Thank you, Tenowk," Valerie said, plopping into her seat. "Thank you, everyone. I'm going to close my eyes for a second. Wake me when we're almost there or I'm about to die. Either works."

It wasn't much later, however, when they woke her.

"You're going to want to see this." Robin nudged her and pointed to the display, which showed a large, lone ship.

Made of a dark metal that nearly blended with the void around it, the ship appeared to be moving slowly, more interested in traveling undetected than getting anywhere quickly.

"What is it?" Valerie asked.

"That's where we traced Rokal to," Flynn replied.

"The prison ship," Jilla said. "SEDE."

Valerie sat up, heart thumping. The unfindable prison ship was right in front of them. They had a chance to save Kalan after all.

CHAPTER NINE

SWARTHIAN EXTENDED DETENTION ENVIRONMENT (SEDE)

Nostro moved through the ship with a practiced speed and agility that forced Kalan and Wearl to move much faster than they had on their previous escape attempts. Kalan figured his confidence came from having every guard on SEDE in his pocket. The Shimmers also manned the security monitors, so they didn't have to worry about being spotted that way.

Nostro led them up another in a long string of ladders. As he climbed, he called back down to Kalan, "So tell me, Grayhewn... Why do you want out of this place so badly?"

The question annoyed Kalan. It was a *prison*. Why did *anyone* want to get out of prison? "Because it totally and complete sucks in here."

Nostro let out a displeased grunt. "That's no answer. Let me put it another way... Your mother is here. The majority of beings you grew up with are here. Not only that, but they are in constant danger. Why are you trying to leave instead of staying here to protect your friends and family?"

Kalan's annoyance threatened to turn to anger. "Perhaps my mother would prefer I spend my life out in the expanse of space living to the fullest rather than huddling in here with her, even if it might make her a tiny bit safer."

"Uh huh. You always do what your mommy tells you?"

Thankfully Wearl spoke before Kalan could lash back at him.

"Let's keep our focus on what we're doing, and refrain from saying things likely to get us punched." She paused for a moment. "Besides, Kalan's mom is the best. *I* do what she tells me, and that's saying a lot."

Nostro chuckled. "Okay, sorry I asked."

Kalan sighed, wondering how bad things had gotten when Wearl was the voice of reason. Something about Nostro's words bothered him, though. Not just that they questioned his integrity, but that there was a hint of truth to them. "You know what? It's actually a fair question. The truth is, I have another family—one outside SEDE. And I believe they need my help more than the people in here do."

Nostro finally reached the top of the ladder and stepped off, shaking the metal deck with the weight of his bulky blue form. "Ah, yes—the Justice Enforcer and her Elites."

Damn, Kalan thought. *Was there anything this guy didn't know?*

"My Shimmers keep me quite well informed of the

happenings in the system, and the Prime Enforcer has certainly been 'happening' recently."

"It's not just them," Kalan told Nostro as he reached the top of the ladder. "You heard of the Lavkin?"

For the first time since Kalan had met him, the big Pallicon looked surprised.

"The Lost Fleet? They've returned?"

Kalan grinned. "Maybe the Shimmers aren't keeping you as up to date as you think."

"They wouldn't keep anything from me—especially something that important."

As soon as he stopped speaking Nostro rocked back on his heels, as if he'd been lightly shoved. Then Wearl spoke, her voice coming from close to Nostro's face. "*Your* Shimmers? I've about had it with you talking about my people like you own them. I want to know why the guards listen to you, and I want to know now!"

Nostro looked at the empty space in front of his face for a long moment, then nodded. He reached down and pulled something from inside his coat. At first glance it looked like a knife and Kalan tensed, but then he realized "knife" wasn't quite the right descriptor. This object was too thick to qualify, and didn't appear very sharp. Looking at it, Kalan had the feeling that it had grown rather than been forged.

"Do you know what this is?" Nostro asked.

There was a long pause, then Wearl answered in a shaky voice. "I know. What can I do to help?"

Nostro smiled. "You're already doing it."

Kalan blinked hard, trying to understand. He'd never heard Wearl sound like that: both afraid and... awed? Her attitude toward Nostro had changed in a split second. "Someone want to catch me up? What is that thing?"

"Should we tell him?" Nostro asked. "Your call."

There was another long pause. "Not now," Wearl finally answered. "It's too much to tell. I'm sorry, Kalan, we'll catch you up later. For now, just know that no Shimmer would ever so much as touch a hair on this Pallicon's head."

"Or my face, hopefully." Nostro ran a hand over the coarse black hairs that stuck out of his face at odd angles, causing them to jiggle wildly. He laughed at Kalan's disgusted expression. "Let's keep moving."

Kalan followed, but his mind remained on what he'd just seen. Wearl had never kept anything from him before, at least to his knowledge. He wondered what that strange object could mean to her and the Shimmers to have made her start keeping secrets now.

Nostro led them to a section of the ship Kalan and Wearl had never seen before. It was on the upper levels, the majority of which were used for guard housing and the engine rooms. Kalan had no idea what type of proof Nostro hoped to find up here.

As if reading his thoughts, Nostro pointed to a darkened doorway up ahead. "This is server room. All the security footage is stored there, including some that Captain Tuttle would prefer no one see."

They stepped through the door and the lights came on, momentarily blinding Kalan. At first, he thought the lights must have been automated, but then he saw Captain Tuttle standing in front of them.

"Footage I'd prefer no one see?" he asked. "That's an

unkind assessment, Nostro. I'm a protector of justice. We don't hide our deeds in the shadows."

"Uh, you were literally just hiding in that shadow," Wearl pointed out.

Tuttle ignored the comment. "Thank you, Kalan and Wearl. I asked you to get Nostro out of the One-Eight-Nine, and you did that."

"Maybe so," Kalan answered, "but we're not handing him over. A few things have changed since last we spoke. I guess you could say the deal's off."

"Yes, it is." The captain smiled at him gently. "I'm afraid there will be no isolation block in your future. No more doing jobs for me, either. I'm going to have to kill you."

Kalan squinted at the small unarmed Skulla, who was standing in front of a Grayhewn, a massive Pallicon, and a perpetually pissed-off Shimmer. "You don't talk like a guy who's facing three enemies alone."

"He's not," Wearl answered. The anger was clear in her voice. "He's got twenty-five Shimmers standing around him."

Tuttle's smile widened. "It took some convincing, but they agreed to help me. I promised I would pardon Nostro for all the infractions he's committed on SEDE, and leave the One-Eight-Nine alone from now on."

Nostro shook his head. "Don't do this."

The deep voice of a male Shimmer answered, "We will protect you no matter the cost, Nostro. That means killing them."

The Pallicon grimaced. "Fine. We'll do it the hard way." He began to grow, his already massive blue body enlarging rapidly. He turned to Kalan and Wearl. "Run!"

Kalan didn't bother arguing; he understood what Nostro was doing. Knowing that the Shimmers wouldn't risk hurting him, he was making himself as large a target as possible—hopefully large enough that the Shimmers wouldn't risk shooting near him.

Pallicons could grow very large, but the physical and mental strain could cause them to spend the next week in bed if they went too far with it. Kalan wouldn't let Nostro's costly defense go to waste. He immediately took off running down the corridor.

"Wearl, you with me?" he shouted as he turned a corner, not daring to look back.

"Here. Running through these damn corridors. Again."

"They say practice makes perfect. Maybe we'll actually escape at some point."

"We'll be lucky to escape with our lives this time."

Commotion and gunfire echoed down the corridor. Kalan thought he must have gotten turned around, since that gunfire wasn't coming from the direction where they'd left Nostro and Tuttle.

"Do you have any idea where we are?" he asked.

Wearl sounded annoyed. "No. I thought you did."

Great. This was going even worse than usual. "We know we're near the top of the ship. Let's find a ladder and climb down."

That turned out to be easier said than done. They ran for another five minutes, turning at random corners; just attempting to go somewhere new in the hope that they'd eventually stumble across a way out of this maze.

Instead, they took another left and found themselves at a dead end.

Wearl let out a frustrated groan. "Now we're definitely lost."

Kalan held up a hand for quiet. He'd heard something—more gunfire, and it appeared to be getting closer.

Chances were not great if the Shimmers cornered them in this dead end, but if he was going down, he was going down shooting.

Then he heard footsteps echoing down the corridor and a voice. "These invisible bastards are a real pain in the ass."

He recognized that voice, but he didn't quite trust his ears. There was no way she could be here. *No possible way.*

Then she rounded the corner.

Valerie.

She was here. The Justice Enforcer herself.

And not just her.

Robin. Bob. Jilla. Flynn. Garcia. Even a couple of beings he didn't recognize.

He lowered his weapon. "*Valerie?*"

She looked equally surprised to see him. "Holy shit. Kalan!"

They all wore shocked expressions, but Bob looked positively flabbergasted. "But...the cellblocks? The guards? How did you get out?"

Kalan couldn't keep the grin off his face. "It's good to see you too, buddy."

Valerie stalked toward him, her expression stern, then grabbed him in a tight hug. "You certainly have a way of attracting trouble."

"*Me?* Wearl and I were just doing my usual try-to-stay-alive-long-enough-to-breakout thing, and somehow you waltz into the most secure prison in the galaxy. How the hell did you get in here?"

Valerie cocked a thumb at Flynn. "This asshole got us in. He explained it, but I stopped paying attention when he started talking about algorithms."

Flynn grinned. "Honestly, it wasn't that tough. You might want to rethink that whole 'most secure prison on the galaxy' thing. All I had to do was hack into the automated system and convince it we were a scheduled delivery, and it let us dock."

Kalan scowled. "I hope this isn't all for me. You have bigger largidations to fry."

"Don't flatter yourself," Robin told him. "We wanted you back, but you're the icing on this cake. And I'm going to pretend I know what a largidation is."

"They're delicious," Wearl answered, "once you remove the poison sack."

Valerie looked around for the source of the voice. "Wearl? I should have known you'd be here. I'd give you a hug if I could see you."

"No, you wouldn't. You'd be too stunned by my hotness."

"Fair enough. By the way, your fellow Shimmers are a giant pain in the ass."

Kalan nodded. "You too? We're dealing with a little Shimmer-related trauma as well."

Valerie glared at Flynn. "Turns out the hacking didn't go as smoothly as some would have us believe."

Flynn's face reddened. "Uh, yeah. Turns out I may have tripped an alarm or two. Funny thing though: the response from the Shimmer guards was sort of lackluster. I would have expected more of them. It was like they were busy or something."

Kalan raised his hand sheepishly. "That may have been partly our fault."

"Not surprising," Valerie replied. "What do you say we walk and talk? I'd rather not be caught in this dead end when the guards *do* show up."

They started down the corridor, Flynn guiding them using a downloaded map on his handheld device. "Should be a straight shot this way."

Kalan nudged Valerie as they walked. "So what brings you here, if it's not to see my pretty face."

Valerie smiled. "I was trying to figure out how to come rescue your ass."

"That's pretty too," Wearl pointed out.

"But we didn't know how to find SEDE. It was dumb luck that we found it at all. We were chasing this Norrul. We think he's working for a freak named Demus. He claims to be a high priest, and he's obsessed with justice. His sick brand of it, anyway."

"Huh." Kalan thought about that. "The way we heard it, the captain of this ship is secretly working for a high priest."

"Guys?" Flynn called. "We need to find an exit strategy. I figure if we—"

The sudden pounding of footsteps racing down the hall interrupted him.

"Shit!" Garcia exclaimed. "They're almost here. Tell me you've got an escape route planned for us, buddy."

Flynn tapped frantically at his device. "Almost got it... Just a minute.... There!" He pointed at a door a little way down the corridor. "It's an engine room. We can cut through there and go deeper into the ship."

"Let's do it," Valerie replied. She dashed for the doorway before anyone else could respond.

Kalan quickly followed. The footsteps seemed to be getting closer, but sounds could be deceptive in these echoing corridors. "Keep an eye out, Wearl."

"On it," the Shimmer replied.

They'd all ducked into the engine room when the gunfire began.

"Um, they're here," Wearl informed them.

Valerie glared at the doorway. "Yeah, I got that. Keep moving, but be ready to fight." She pulled a gun out of a holster on her belt and slapped it into Kalan's hand. "Here. My gift to you."

His eyes lit up. "A Tralen-14!"

"Once we realized this was SEDE, I grabbed one from the crate on the *Grandeur* in case we ran into you. Now let's get moving."

They raced through the room, dodging equipment and control panels. Kalan knew smaller spacecraft, but he'd never been exposed to engines of this size. He had no idea what any of this stuff was.

"They're coming through the doorway," Wearl announced.

The sound of gunfire filled the air immediately.

Valerie stopped running. "Shit! Now's our chance. Fire at that doorway. We may not be able to see them, but we know they have to squeeze through that opening."

Valerie's Elites, together again, opened fire, causing

absolute devastation to anything trying to pass through the doorway.

"We're taking out a bunch of them!" Wearl shouted. "Keep at it."

Still the gunfire from the Shimmers continued.

A round struck something behind Flynn and an alarm began to blare.

"I'm suddenly regretting having a firefight in the engine room," he remarked.

Valerie glared at him, annoyed. "That thing's not important, is it?"

Flynn looked at the damaged machinery for a moment, then went pale. "Uh, I don't know how to tell you this, Valerie, but it's pretty important."

"Define important," Kalan shouted.

Flynn grimaced. "It controls the navigation, so I'd say it's very damn important. And if I'm not mistaken, that blaring alarm means our current flightpath is on a collision course with something very large."

"Hold your fire!" a voice Kalan recognized as Captain Tuttle's ordered, and the Shimmers immediately stopped shooting.

"Don't listen to whoever the hell that was," Valerie ordered. "Keep shooting!"

"Shooting at what?" Flynn asked.

Valerie shrugged. "Fair point."

"Prime Enforcer!" Captain Tuttle called through the doorway. "May we speak?"

Kalan looked at Valerie. "'Prime Enforcer?' That's what you're going by now?"

"The grander the name, the fewer people I have to kill."

She raised her voice and shouted toward the door, "We can talk, but leave your invisible lackeys outside. Wearl, keep him honest."

"On it," Wearl agreed.

Captain Tuttle marched through the doorway, hands raised and an easy smile on his face.

Valerie raised an eyebrow as the diminutive Skulla entered. "This is the big bad captain of SEDE?"

"Neither big nor bad," Tuttle answered. "Just a creature out for justice. Much like yourself, I'm told."

Valerie sighed. "Seems like everybody's out for justice today, but nobody knows what it really means."

That reminded Kalan of something. "Where's Nostro, Captain?"

The Skulla's smile wavered, but only for a moment. "He's where he belongs. Don't worry about him."

Kalan balled his fists. He wanted nothing more than to punch this little Skulla in the face, but he reminded himself that this guy had control of the ship. It was better to let this play out.

"My very good friend has asked me not to harm you Prime Enforcer. He thinks you could be useful."

"Yeah?" Valerie asked. "Who's your friend? I like him already."

"High Priest Demustrius."

Valerie frowned. "Actually, scratch that. I've met that guy, and I wasn't a fan."

"The way I see it, you have two choices."

"This guy and his 'two choices,'" Wearl muttered.

Tuttle ignored the comment. "Come with me, and we will travel in comfort on our way to see the high priest. Or you can hope you survive the crash."

Kalan raised an eyebrow. "Crash."

"You didn't know? SEDE is a modular ship. If one section is too badly damaged—or say it catches fire—it can be jettisoned to protect the rest of the ship."

"Sorry, I don't follow why you're telling us this," Valerie said.

Tuttle grinned. "You hear that alarm? That's the ship letting us know this portion of the ship is in danger of detaching. So if you don't take my offer, you'd better hope there're enough seats for all of you in the emergency crash room—not that there's much chance of that saving you. My Shimmers will make sure you can't leave this part of the ship. I've programmed this section to rocket toward the nearest planet when it detaches, though I warn you, the landing won't be comfortable."

Kalan's eyes widened. "No way. You'd let part of the ship be destroyed simply to kill us? What about the prisoners in this section?"

"There's only one cellblock in this section, and it's a small one. Only a few dozen prisoners would be killed. They probably deserve it anyway."

Kalan took a step forward. "You son of a bitch."

Wearl cleared her throat. "Um, guys, they're flanking us. Shimmers are gathering outside each door."

"Last chance, Prime Enforcer," Tuttle cooed, that dumb smile still on his face. "Are you going to join me, or are you going down with the ship?"

Valerie began to draw her sword. "If *we're* going down with the ship, so are you."

CHAPTER TEN

SWARTHIAN EXTENDED DETENTION ENVIRONMENT (SEDE)

Alarms were blaring and the shouting of Shimmer guards came from all directions, mostly discussing abandoning this section of the ship. One was arguing, however, and it seemed some were agreeing.

"Get ready," Valerie called, gesturing that direction.

"No, to the right," Wearl argued. "I saw them coming from that way. Others."

"Shit, so...both directions?" Robin asked.

"Right."

Valerie glanced back. "We need to get to the emergency crash room."

"Us, and anyone else left on this chunk o' junk," Garcia said, eyes wide as he moved his rifle from passage to passage.

"Wide eyes won't help you see us," Wearl noted.

"Shut up and tell us where they are!"

"Right, in three, two…" She paused. "Shoot now!"

Everyone took cover and opened up. Valerie unloaded before turning back to Flynn and saying, "You and Wearl cover the other route. Fall back on my command." She fired some more, only able to guess where to shoot based on the curses and shouts coming from the enemy Shimmers.

"AHHH!" Flynn started firing on the other passage, despite Wearl shouting that there wasn't an enemy.

Suddenly Wearl called, "Oh, damn. Keep shooting! You got one, but there are three more!"

"How we doing over here?" Valerie asked, pulling back and noting that there was no more talking or shouting from the various passages.

There was a thud and Wearl grunted, then something hit the floor.

"Wearl?" Kalan asked, worried.

"I'm fine," Wearl assured him. "There was one left. None now."

"Good, now get us to the damn emergency room," Valerie yelled.

"Behind you. Stay close." They heard footsteps, then Wearl told them, "Just go. I'll tell you when to turn."

They ran, careful not to go too fast and take the lead, pausing at times to wait for Wearl to give them directions. Several prisoners ran by, and Wearl explained that the cells had likely opened in the malfunction.

As they turned a corner, they saw something unexpected—a Norrul with a metallic carapace.

"Rokal!" Valerie shouted in surprise.

The Norrul looked just as surprised to see them. He

held something in his hand: a glowing orb. It had to be what he'd taken from the male he'd shot in the ruins of Silahu Corporation's compound. When he laid eyes on Valerie, he clutched it to his chest.

"Captain Tuttle!" he shouted, looking back the way he'd come. "They're over here! We must protect the orb!"

Valerie and Robin glanced at each other.

"We're definitely taking that orb now, right?" Robin asked.

Valerie smiled. She knew they didn't have long. They'd have to get to that emergency crash room fast. "Leave it to me. Get the others to safety."

She sprinted toward the Norrul and slammed into him. The force of the impact knocked the orb lose, and it rolled across the deck.

"That belongs to Captain Tuttle," Rokal snarled. He swung his big arm and the back of his hand connected with the side of Valerie's head, sending her stumbling backward.

He reached for the orb, unaware that Valerie had already recovered from his blow. Her foot slammed into his back and he went sprawling to the deck.

She scooped up the orb. Rokal was trying to struggle to his feet, but the blaring alarms reminded Valerie that she didn't have time to continue this fight. Instead, she turned and dashed after her friends.

When she reached the emergency room, Wearl was guiding them to the seats. She came face to face with a heavy alien who resembled about three Arlays in one and had a metal arm. The alien glared, then pointed away.

"How bad are most of these prisoners?" Valerie asked Kalan.

"Aside from me, you mean?" he replied. "Most of them are the worst of the worst. Imagine something truly horrible, and I'm guessing this guy did it."

"That's all I wanted to hear," she said and stepped forward, socking the alien in the stomach. The alien doubled over, but four more ran at them—three up front and one toward the back who'd been stuck trying to unfasten himself but was now free.

"Get out of our way," Kalan shouted, holding out his hands. "There's plenty of room for all of us in there."

"Problem is, we've got friends coming," one of them explained, squaring off against Kalan. "And you hit my pal here."

"Wasn't me." Kalan gestured to Valerie.

"Her?" The alien barked a laugh, then glared at Kalan. "Nah, no way she could've done that to Bonbon."

"'Bonbon?'" Robin asked, laughing. "And what's your name, 'Plum Pudding?'"

The alien glared at her but shook his head, the joke going right over him. "No, it's Anwan."

"Dondon, Pompom, and whatever the fuck your names are," Robin began, stepping up to him. "Get out of our way, or learn how hard a little girl can hit."

Anwan spread his arms wide. "Give it your best shot."

Valerie stepped toward Robin to pull her back, then glanced at Anwan. "Actually, yeah, give him hell."

Anwan grinned...until Robin's punch sent waves across his ample belly and he flew back to crash against the far wall.

"Get them out of here," Valerie ordered, tossing one of them down the hall. The others got the rest of the aliens out and followed her into the room, where they found a series of chairs along the walls and more in rows, all with crash harnesses.

The ship was falling through Rhol's atmosphere, and there wasn't a damn thing any of them could do about it. After securing the door behind them, Valerie used her strength to help others to the seats and strap them in, figuring that was their best chance for survival. A glance through the only window in the room showed other ships out there, likely more from the Demus's fleet. Lolack's fleet had drawn some of them off, but more were coming. Apparently this was their staging ground, which wasn't good news for Valerie and her team.

"We're all going to die!" Bob cried, leaning over and putting his head in his hands.

"Probably," Valerie replied. "So don't be a wuss. At least make it fun."

"*WHAT?*"

"Like me...joking around," she told him as she found a spot to strap herself in. "Maybe I'll laugh the whole way down, just for kicks."

"Valerie," Robin said.

"Yeah?"

"SHUT UP!"

Valerie laughed, but since they were all glaring, she stopped and pretended to zip her mouth.

"They're harsh," Kalan admitted, glancing out the window. "I mean, you did come to rescue me, even if it ended up leading to my death."

"See? Humor," Valerie said, but he wasn't smiling. Okay, time to change her tone. "Listen, everyone," she started, only to be interrupted by a loud *crash* and vibration as part of the ship tore off from the rest. "We're not going to die!"

"How do you know?" Robin asked.

"Because that crazy Demus guy is still out there, and I haven't had a chance to put my size-seven Puma up his ass. Or these armor boot-things."

"I love the optimism!" Jilla stated, and started laughing. It didn't sound right coming from her, but then Flynn joined in and Valerie couldn't help it. She hadn't been serious, but why not? The ship spun then, giving them a view of the clay-like ground that was rising up fast.

"Brace for impact!" she shouted and then they'd landed, everything rattling and shaking. The ship broke apart and there was a deafening *crack*, and she was out.

Lucky her...she healed fast. If something had hit her head the effect wouldn't last, and soon she was looking around and blinking.

The ship was torn up, wires dangling and long pieces of metal sticking out here and there. It was dark but for the sparks and lines of orange light streaming in from outside. Robin, groaned, pulling herself free from a piece of metal wall that had broken off and pierced her shoulder. It looked like it hurt like hell, but that wouldn't last long.

"Everyone alive?" Kalan asked, pushing himself to his feet and moving a broken portion of the ceiling out of his way.

"Check those next to you," Valerie said, turning away from Robin to see that Flynn was still unconscious. Not dead; she was glad to verify he was breathing, so she gently got him out of the harness. When she laid him on the floor, he started groaning and gradually came around.

Garcia had a large bump on his head and Jilla stumbled at first, but everyone seemed to be in pretty good shape. By the time she'd checked everyone, Flynn was pale and holding his head, but on his feet.

"We've got to move," Valerie said, glancing around to locate the best way out of there. She saw more orange light than elsewhere coming through a crack in the wall to their right, so she figured they'd try that. "They'll be after us soon, and judging from our last visit to this planet, the locals might not be on our side."

"What did you do to them?" Kalan asked, already moving in the direction she'd indicated.

"Showed our faces. Apparently that was enough."

"I have to give you credit," he told her, stopping to shove a control terminal out of their way. "I'm still alive."

"And I mean to see that you stay that way," she replied, guiding the others toward the exit.

When they exited the ship, her worries were confirmed. Already transport ships were descending toward them, and there was more: some of the other prisoners had survived and were already moving out, though half of them were stuck in the clay surface.

"Grab sheet metal from the debris," Valerie commanded, already at work. "Anything we can use to cover the ground as we move across it."

They followed her orders without question, and soon had a good walkway across the clay. Others saw this and did the same, while some on the ship started making their way over to follow them.

When they reached the edge of the clay and the beginning of the orange bushes someone started firing at them, but the shots went wide.

Valerie glanced back to see Captain Tuttle, but she didn't waste much time on him.

"They're going to be coming after us; hunting us down, if possible," she said. "We need to find cover and a place to hide."

"I say we risk it with the Norrul," Robin declared. "We don't know for sure they betrayed us."

"Who else would've called in Demus's fleet?" Garcia countered.

Valerie scanned the area, searching for an alternative but finding none. "He's right, but you both are. There's nowhere else to hide."

"So we hand ourselves over to them?" Robin asked as they entered the vegetated area, doing their best to move quickly as more shots came. The bushes were prickly and reached out as if they were alive.

"No, we find a way in without them knowing," Valerie replied.

Kalan laughed. "I'm not exactly...you know...*inconspicuous*."

"But one of us is," Jilla pointed out.

"Ah, Wearl."

Everyone froze and Kalan called, "Wearl?"

"Yes?" Wearl's voice came from behind Valerie.

"Can you look for a way in that won't get us noticed."

"One step ahead of you," she said, sneaking past, "but a word of caution. The others are starting to round up the prisoners, so let's hurry this up."

"All on you," Valerie said.

"Any coming after *us* yet?" Kalan asked. They saw a group of escapees getting pushed to the ground by invisible guards in the distance.

Silence followed for a moment, then Wearl said, "No, but keep down while I'm finding us a way in. Don't move until I'm back."

They did their best to get under the bushes and out of sight, and stayed still. Valerie and a few others still wore their battle armor, but not Kalan.

"How's your shoulder?" Valerie asked Robin in a whisper. They were side by side, and when she turned her head she could see herself in her friend's eyes through her faceplate.

"It's healing up well. Almost done, I think."

"I'm glad it missed your heart."

Robin frowned. "Think that would've mattered? I mean, would a wound like that kill us?"

Valerie shrugged. "I've actually never asked the one person I think would know, and I haven't experimented, so...good question."

For a moment they lay there, and then Robin held out her hand. Valerie took it and tilted her head, confused.

Squeezing it softly, Robin smiled and said, "We're going to get through this," before withdrawing her hand again. For a moment Valerie had thought maybe there had been more to the gesture, but judging by the worried look in Robin's eyes, that wouldn't have made sense. This was a time for them to run for their lives, not hold hands and bat eyelashes at each other.

"As soon as the captain gets out of there he'll send the

guards in our direction," Jilla pointed out.

"Not to worry," came Wearl's voice. "We have an in."

"You're a lifesaver," Valerie whispered. "Show us the way."

"Follow my voice," Wearl replied, then started making low tsking sounds as she moved. The rest crawled out from under the bushes and followed in a crouched run.

She led them to the side of the metal pillars, from which location they saw a group of Norrul running toward the crash site. Whether they were going to help or fight escaped prisoners, they were best avoided for now.

After more tsking, Valerie saw an unguarded opening near the back of one of the wider pillars. The group moved toward it, pausing only once as more Norrul passed by two rows over. As the group ducked in Valerie stood aside, wanting to be ready in case there was trouble and she needed to cover them. Her eyes wandered over the natural stairs within the tower, which looked as if someone had simply told the metal what to do and it had listened. How anyone could have built this was beyond her.

Once everyone was in she cautiously entered and went up two steps...and found herself staring straight into the eyes of a young Norrul. The small girl looked almost like a human, her carapace barely formed except for low ridges around her collarbone, which were visible through the nightgown she wore.

"I'm not going to hurt anyone," Valerie whispered, slowly moving back.

"They didn't mean it," the girl said, eyeing Valerie sadly.

"What?"

"The others. I heard them talking and debating... When

they called *him*, they didn't have a choice."

Valerie nodded, understanding that she must be referring to Moralu calling down this Demus character and his fleet.

"Are you safe?" Valerie asked.

The little girl grunted. "Yes, but if they hadn't told him and he had found out... Others serve him. Others would have told on us."

"I understand," Valerie replied, turning to leave. "I'm not mad."

"You'll stop him?"

Valerie stopped in her tracks, turned back, and nodded. "He scares you?"

"I have nightmares."

"Those nightmares won't go on much longer, I promise." Valerie gave her a smile, then turned and followed her friends below, more determined than ever to find a way to defeat Demus and his fleet.

They found themselves in another large room, similar to the one in which the so-called celebrations had been held earlier. This room's metal walls were less finely formed, as if the being shaping them had been practicing. In areas the metal jutted out like arms or legs, and on one wall it looked like someone had made a large face.

"How are they doing this?" Garcia asked, tracing his hand along the metal. "It's all one piece, not welded together."

Flynn chuckled. "Let's hang around for a bit so they can capture us, and we can ask them. Or, we can keep moving."

"Shut up." Garcia turned to Valerie. "When did he become Mr. Jokes?"

But she was still too focused on thoughts of the little girl and what sort of person Demus must be if he inspired such fear. She just shrugged. The others felt her mood and became silent as well, which was smart considering their predicament.

It wasn't long before the first of them had to relieve themselves, so they took a break at a section of tunnels and, feeling bad about it, used a side tunnel to take turns. They found a spot to rest for a few minutes, which was even more necessary because they didn't have water or food.

"Finally," Flynn griped, stretching his legs.

Robin went to each of them to check for injuries, careful to not bump into Wearl.

"How'd we find ourselves in the middle of this war between two large fleets?" Valerie asked when the younger woman came over to her.

"And neither side is Earth," Robin replied with a laugh. "But at least Lolack would make a good ally."

Valerie nodded. "Anyone willing to hurt innocents in their quest for justice is wrong. It brings on more injustice and a new round of people seeking their own revenge."

"We're on the right side here, no doubt about it," Robin assured her, then left to check on Flynn and Garcia.

"It's never easy." Kalan glanced at her from his place against the wall. With his gray skin, it almost looked like he was part of the metal.

"What's that?"

"Choosing sides. Figuring out who the real allies are." He grunted. "I wasn't even fully sure about you until recently."

"You're joking!"

"Maybe. I knew you were trustworthy right away, but think about it... You just showed up and took over the transport ship, then convinced me to kind of break the rules to get you into a death fight. The Damu Michezo. Are those the signs of someone you should trust?"

"Huh. Good point!"

"And then you destroyed the Damu Michezo," he continued, "and risked your life to help against Aranaught. You know, when she was still an enemy. All that made me see you in a different light."

"Sometimes we have to do things that don't seem right," she admitted. "I think it's the moment you allow innocents to get hurt that separates the evil from the just."

"I agree. Do the ends justify the means? Only if evil wasn't done to achieve those means."

She assessed Kalan, then smiled. "You know, I don't think I've told you yet how much I appreciate you."

He laughed. "No need for that."

"No, no." She stood, walked over, and took his hand as if the shake it. "There need to be more like you in the universe. How many times would we have been helpless without you?"

"Helpless? Probably zero," he demurred. "You would've found a way."

She shrugged. "Maybe, maybe not. Point is, you're great."

She let go of his hand and was about to go over to see if Robin needed help when a gleam of metal caught her eye.

"Did you notice that?" Robin asked, pointing the other way.

Valerie hopped to her feet. "Go! The walls are moving."

The others began to rise, but clearly her words had inspired more confusion than reaction. They were all trying to see if the walls were indeed moving. There was no time for watching so Valerie led the charge, motioning them along and grabbing Flynn by the arm and pulling him with her. Kalan was beside her, and together they held a wall back when it tried to close before half the group was through.

They made it through and fell back as the metal slammed together, and sure enough the tunnels ahead were moving too, changing direction right before their eyes.

"Just go!" she said to the others, who were looking at her and Kalan hesitantly. "We have to find a way out."

They kept running, but the tunnels appeared to be moving back around. All passages led back to Demus, she imagined. As much as she wanted to find out how this was done, getting out of there was more important.

At the next tunnel she decided to try something. With all her strength, she ran at the metal and kicked, breaking right through. Of course, they were in another tunnel and the far wall was moving too, but at least she now knew that the metal wasn't very thick.

They followed her through a few more tunnels in this fashion, until they heard voices behind them. Turning to see Rokal, Valerie watched with awe as he put his hand to the wall and his metal carapace vibrated. A moment later the walls started forming layers around Valerie and her team.

If she didn't act fast, they'd be trapped.

"Robin, on me!" she said, and they ran to the far side, kicking and punching their way through metal walls. The others joined them and started pushing, but suddenly there was a yelp behind them and Valerie saw that Jilla had been cut off from the group.

Valerie tried to punch back through, but more walls warped inward, nearly catching Kalan. He pushed back, his strength almost enough to hold it back. Valerie fought to get to him, but the metal was moving in on her now too.

"Get help!" he shouted. "Find a way out. We'll figure this out!"

She wasn't about to let them go so easily, but the walls kept coming and Robin pulled her back.

"He's right!" Robin said, holding her close, nose inches from her own. "It doesn't do the team any good if we're all captured."

Valerie shook her off and kept pushing through walls. At one wall, the metal gave way to reveal green skin and wide eyes—Jilla!

She ran to Valerie and Robin, happy to see them, then glanced around. "Kalan? The others?"

"We can't leave them!"

"We won't," Valerie assured her.

Garcia stumbled in on them and fell to his knees, and they helped him to stand. "We can't hold out like this," he said, eyes wide and searching. "Where's Flynn?"

"We'll find them," Valerie said, continuing the fight even as more walls pushed them back, making it seem more hopeless by the minute.

CHAPTER ELEVEN

PLANET RHOL

Kalan slammed his hand against the metal wall of the tunnel. "I can't believe this! We reunite with Valerie for, what, twenty minutes? Now we're cut off from her again?"

"Metal tunnels," Wearl noted. "Exactly like home."

Flynn's face was pale as he stared down the tunnel they were in. "So I'm with you guys now? Normally I roll with Valerie."

"Yeah, well, normally we end up with Bob, so I guess we'll consider you an upgrade."

Kalan took a deep breath. He needed to get it together. Part of SEDE had just broken off, and they'd crashed to this strange planet. He had to assume most of the prisoners had died in the crash, as well as most of the guards. Only a few dozen in that part of the ship, Captain Tuttle had said, but every lost life was a tragedy. He could hardly imagine how scary and confusing their last few minutes must have been. They had been going about their normal day in their cellblock, when all of a sudden the world started spinning. And a few minutes later, they'd crashed into a planet they hadn't even known they were falling toward.

He tried to push those thoughts away. Wearl and Flynn needed him. Valerie needed him. And Captain Tuttle needed a punch in the face—one Kalan would be more than happy to provide.

Down the tunnel they heard echoing footsteps, as well as a strange dragging sound.

"I suddenly regret pounding on the wall," Kalan muttered.

Flynn nodded. "Probably not the best idea, considering we have the captain of a prison ship and an army of invisible guards after us."

"Not to mention the creepy locals," Wearl added.

Kalan's hand went to his weapon. "Let's just be ready."

They waited in silence as the footsteps grew closer, preparing for the fight they knew was coming. After a moment, a large shape darkened the entrance to the tunnel.

Kalan couldn't help but smile as he recognized the being approaching them.

Flynn raised a shaky finger. "Um, big ugly blue guy. Should we be shooting at him?"

"Nah," Kalan said. "He's a new friend. Glad to see you're alive, Nostro. We didn't know what Captain Tuttle did to you."

"Threw me in a closet was what he did," the Pallicon explained. "Said it was for my own protection, so the Shimmers would help him. Let's just say it was not a comfortable landing." He looked at Flynn. "I don't mind being called ugly, but I do mind you not helping me with my buddy here."

He angled his large body to the left and Kalan saw that he was dragging someone along with him; an injured person.

Kalan and Flynn ran to help as soon as the saw the prisoner, a young, Skulla male. They laid him gently on the ground.

Nostro crouched next to them. "What do you think? Is he going to make it?"

Kalan observed the teen Skulla's shallow breathing and the massive wound on his head. "I'm no doctor." That was the most positive thing he could say.

They waited in silence, tending the Skulla's wound as best they could, but within a few moments, he'd taken his last breath.

Kalan put a hand on Nostro's should. "I'm sorry."

Nostro brushed the hand off and got to his feet. "It's not you who should be sorry, it's Captain Tuttle. When I catch him, I'm going to make him pay."

"That's what I was thinking too," Kalan agreed.

"I dug through that rubble for twenty minutes near where the cellblock must have been, and this guy was the only one I found. The Shimmers must have gotten the rest." He slammed his hand against the wall, and it clanged even more loudly than when Kalan had done the same thing.

"Really?" Flynn asked. "Again with the wall-hitting? Have we learned nothing?"

If Nostro heard the comment, he gave no indication.

Kalan glanced down the tunnel, wondering who else

might have heard the noise. "We'll make Captain Tuttle pay, but I think we should get moving."

They headed down the tunnel in silence. Each time they came to a fork, Kalan took the righthand turn—not out of any sort of knowledge of the tunnel system, but simply because it took the choice out of it and let them keep moving quickly.

They'd been walking for ten minutes when Wearl said, "Hang on, I heard something."

The group froze, and sure enough…a few minutes later a figure appeared. It was a Norrul female, but she had no metal carapace. This one looked more like the standard variety Kalan had been seeing all his life.

The female blinked hard when she saw them. "What are you doing down here?"

"We're trying to get out of here," Kalan said softly. He had often found when encountering strangers, even big Norrul, he needed to work hard to come off as non-threatening.

She looked at them for a long moment. "The only way out is through."

"Huh." Flynn scoffed. "I think I saw that engraved on a plaque or something once. Very inspirational."

The Norrul looked Kalan in the eye. "Keep going down this tunnel. Every turn, take the way that leads deeper into the ground."

"Deeper? That's the way out?"

She nodded. "It's the fastest way, but it's also the most dangerous. Be careful not to wake him."

"Him?" Nostro asked. "Him who?"

"The Ravagion. He's hungry when he wakes up."

Flynn raised a hand. "Um, is there maybe a slower way that doesn't have a sleeping Ravage-thingie?"

"Once you're past the Ravagion, follow the tunnels that lead upward. I'm sorry, I have to go. They're trying to find me." With that, she squeezed past them and took off running the way Kalan and the others had come.

"Well, that was cryptic," Wearl declared.

Kalan started down the tunnel again. "At least we have some direction now. We'll just be careful. No more hitting walls, and limited talking—then we won't wake the Ravage-guy."

They continued walking, proceeding as quietly as possible. The next three forks they came to, they took the path that sloped downward. The farther they went, the less they heard the echoes of the city from behind them. The air began to smell of dirt, but there was also a coppery metallic component to the scent.

Then they went a long time without any forks.

"We've got to be getting near the end of this thing, right?" Flynn whispered.

"I hope so," Kalan replied. "At least we're starting to get some variety in the view."

Up ahead, the tunnel widened from the original ten feet to at least thirty. It was difficult to tell an exact measurement, because the metal on the walls and floor were covered with orange clay.

When they reached the last of the clay, they stopped and looked ahead. Looking down, they could see a large hole in the floor of the tunnel. It was as if something had burrowed through the metal into the orange clay below.

"Huh," Nostro said. "Do you think this is the Ravage-doo-hickey that Norrul was talking—"

A creature the same color as the clay leaped out of the hole and landed on the floor in front of them on all fours, where it stood snarling.

"Holy shit," Flynn muttered. "I'm going to go out on a limb and say that's the Ravagion."

The creature was twenty feet tall at the shoulder, and it was covered in shiny orange scales. Its face was dominated by a long, pointed snout. The thing's eyes appeared to be too small for its head, but its oversized sharp teeth made up for them.

The Ravagion took a tiny step forward, and its scales rippled in the tunnel's soft light.

Kalan stepped forward, drawing his weapon, but a hand on his arm held him back.

"Let Nostro handle this one," Wearl told him.

Kalan was surprised. Wearl had never had anything but confidence in him before. "Really?"

"It's nothing against you. He has experience with this type of thing. Right, Nostro?"

The Pallicon took a hesitant step forward. "Well, not *this* type of thing exactly, but similar. I got this."

Kalan and Flynn exchanged a glance. It sounded like Nostro was trying to talk himself into this.

"Okay, be my guest," Kalan said. He stood back and watched, considering how he would handle such an intimidating opponent. It seemed to him that its small eyes indicated that it had a limited field of vision. If you could get around the thing, you might have a chance. You just needed to avoid its mouth with those rows of teeth and you'd be fine.

Nostro charged directly at the creature's mouth.

"What are you doing?" Flynn shouted.

But it was too late. Nostro was committed to his attack. The Pallicon raised his weapon but the Ravagion swung his huge snout, easily knocking him aside.

Nostro fell to the floor and slid backward on his ass.

The Ravagion took a step toward him.

Kalan moved to join the fight, but once again Wearl held him back.

"What are you doing?" he growled at her. "This doesn't have to be a one-on-one fight."

Wearl snapped back at him immediately, "Nostro knows what he's doing against a creature like this. You're going to have to trust me."

Kalan hesitantly stepped back. He wasn't a fan of letting his friends tackle a fight alone when he was perfectly capable of helping, but he trusted Wearl. He'd hang back, since she said it was the right move.

Nostro struggled to his feet, and took a few steps back. That was promising. At least he was trying to put some distance between him and the creature. Then he could shoot at it and—

The Pallicon once again charged forward, right at the snout.

Flynn shook his head. "This guy really wants to get eaten by a giant armadillo monster."

Nostro had just about reached it when the Ravagion lowered its snout and snapped it up, slamming it into Nostro's chest and sending him flying backward.

The Pallicon landed hard, and this time it took him a bit longer to stand. "I'm all right. I got this."

Kalan looked at the creature, whose expression was quickly transforming from curious to pissed. "Wearl, let me help. We can do this as a team. There's no reason he has to face it alone."

"Yes, there is," Wearl hissed at him. For the first time, there was a bit of hesitation in her voice.

This time Nostro stood at a distance and fired at the creature. The ammunition ricocheted off its scaly armor, and Kalan tried to figure out what the Pallicon was aiming at. Kalan would have gone for the eyes or even the nostrils; anything unprotected by those scales. Nostro, however, appeared to be firing almost randomly at its body.

It his goal was to leave it uninjured and severely pissed off, then his plan was succeeding wildly.

The Ravagion shook itself and began ambling toward Nostro. Because it was so big it didn't appear to be moving that fast, but it was definitely closing the gap quickly.

Nostro held his ground, gun raised and still firing at the armor.

"Okay, screw this," Kalan muttered. He charged forward before Wearl could stop him.

The Ravagion opened his mouth and the tunnel's light gleamed off its long pointed teeth. It angled its snout sideways and reached forward, ready to grab Nostro in its gaping maw.

Kalan reached the Pallicon first. He slammed into Nostro, wrapping his arms around him and tackling him to the ground.

The Ravagion's mouth missed them by inches.

Kalan quickly sprang to his feet. "Everyone! Let's surround this thing while we have it distracted."

Flynn nodded and darted to the far wall to make his way to the tunnel beyond. Given the creature's small eyes, he anticipated no problem getting past the Ravagion unseen. All Kalan had to do was keep himself and Nostro alive while they distracted it.

He hoped Wearl had been smart enough to follow Flynn around the creature, but he highly doubted it. She was never one to turn away from a fight, even when doing so would have been the right move.

Kalan considered the Ravagion. They didn't have to kill it, simply get past it. Now that he'd seen it attack a few times, it was clear the thing was predictable.

Kalan grabbed Nostro's arm. "Follow me!"

The two of them charged at the creature's right side.

The Ravagion turned its snout toward them and let out an angry snarl.

"It lowers its snout before it attacks," Kalan shouted. "Get ready to jump!"

Nostro tensed. "*What?*"

There was no time to explain further.

As the Ravagion lunged at them, Kalan leaped into the air. The monster brought its snout up under Kalan just as he'd hoped. He was suddenly standing on the creature's nose.

He was relieved to see Nostro right behind him when he glanced over his shoulder.

"Come on!" Kalan called. He raced up the slope of the creature's snout past its eyes and onto the top of its head.

The Ravagion gave a violent shake and Kalan almost

toppled off, but Nostro grabbed on his shoulder, steadying him.

The two large guys charged down the creature's back.

The creature shook again, this time succeeding in knocking them off, but thankfully they'd already reached the tail. They hit the floor on the other side of the pit, where Flynn was waiting for them. He quickly helped them to their feet and all three ran beyond the clay and into the tunnel.

The Ravagion let out a frustrated howl, but it appeared unwilling to go past the edge of the clay to where they were standing.

"Holy *shit*! That was intense," Flynn panted.

"Wearl," Kalan called. "Did you make it?"

There was no response for a moment, then Nostro stumbled backward as something unseen slammed into his chest.

"You ass!" Wearl shouted.

"Wearl, calm down," Kalan said. "What's wrong?"

"This son of a bitch is what's wrong. He showed me the Borin's Tooth. He's supposed to be a great monster fighter, and yet he proved he has no idea what he's doing!"

Flynn furrowed his brow. "Um, are you and confused as I am, Kalan?"

"Yes. You're going to have to explain, Wearl."

Nostro sighed. His eyes were on his feet. "Maybe I should be the one to explain. I owe you an apology. I'm not a great monster fighter. I'm a liar. Let me tell you the story of what happened in the six months after I aged out of SEDE."

CHAPTER TWELVE

PLANET RHOL

They'd been running through tunnels trying to find Kalan and the others for what seemed like hours. There was no indication of time passing down here, only the burning frustration at having been separated again so soon after reuniting. Every turn resulted in more moving walls, more confusion, and more exasperation.

"We're not leaving without them," Jilla said, voice quavering as they reached the outskirts of the city.

Their current tunnel had opened into a sort of underground jungle, then its moving metal closed behind them. Ahead the ground curved down, and there were massive vines and strange black foliage hanging from the earth above. Intermittent holes down the length pf the tunnel let in light.

"Not a chance," Valerie agreed, but we're also not staying here. "We'll find a way through, then work our way back up and..." Even she was feeling the hopelessness of the situation.

"You all are too afraid to say it," Garcia stated. "With all the forces up there, our best bet is to reach Lolack through Tenowk and rain down hell until we find Kalan."

"And the others," Robin added, with a glance toward Jilla.

"It pisses me off too," Garcia assured them. "Flynn has become like a brother to me, but if we were in the same boat, we'd want them to get help. If we can get back to them without it, sure, but trapping ourselves down here without Lolack's fleet knowing how to find us—"

"And how do you propose we contact them?" Jilla asked, spinning on him.

"High ground," he said.

"You think the jamming of our signals is related to the metal here?" Valerie asked hopefully. Since they'd been separated from their team each of them had tried numerous times to reach out, as well as reaching out to Tenowk and the fleet, but nothing had worked.

He shrugged. "If not, we're relying on luck."

"The fleet will come back for us," Jilla insisted.

"Maybe, maybe not." Valerie hated to admit that. "We've always been resourceful. They have a mission, and just because they haven't heard from us in a bit doesn't mean they'll assume the worst. Even if they did, they wouldn't know exactly where to find us, and the rest of Demus's fleet is likely following between them and us."

Everyone took a moment to let that sink in, but their break was interrupted by shouting to their left. Figures blocked the light as they climbed down, and there was an eruption of gunfire when someone saw them.

"Can't stay here," Valerie said, gesturing her crew on. They slid down the metallic hill they were on and found solid ground beneath them, covered in the strange vines and other odd forms of plant life.

Shadows flittered across the beams of light from above, and they could hear the aircraft engines and shouting, followed by shots and explosions. Clearly there was a fight going on, but was it the escaped prisoners or someone else?

That Lolack's fleet would've already shown up seemed too much to a hope, but maybe the prisoners' fighting would be enough to distract the enemy long enough for Kalan and the others to escape. As far she knew they weren't prisoners either, and would be working their way out of the maze.

As they progressed through the strange terrain they found spots where the ground had sunk in and others where the roots and growing plants were too dense to walk through, so they had to make their way around.

After some time they reached a section of ground that went up at an angle, with enough plants along it that they figured everyone could climb. Garcia volunteered to take the lead and check above.

"How're we doing?" Valerie asked Robin, as they waited for him.

"Healed up. Anxious."

"We're going to find them."

Robin stared at Garcia, who was nearly at the top. "Remember how much easier this was back home?"

"You thought that was *easy?*" Valerie scoffed.

"Well, no. But compared to being stranded on an alien planet with a fleet of enemy ships surrounding us and invisible prison guards running around up there, I'd say this is a relative shitnado."

"What?"

"You know, like a tornado meets a shit-storm. 'Shitnado.'"

Valerie laughed and glanced at Jilla and Bob, who were chatting. "It might've been easier, but this is more exciting. I mean, would you go back to those days, not knowing what was out here? Not knowing who was fighting the battle for us?"

"Is this for us?" Robin countered, eyes moving to her now.

"Of course it is. The Alliance—"

"I get the big picture," Robin interrupted. "But right now I'm thinking about my parents and the immediate. Is this really for *us*, or for three generations from now?"

"I honestly don't know." Valerie watched Garcia as he disappeared into the light above, waiting to see if he'd give a signal. After a moment she said, "You'd rather go back to Michael and Bethany Anne? Be part of that fight?"

They locked eyes as Robin considered the thought.

"No?" Valerie prodded.

"Only with you."

"I can't leave anything undone."

"But if we're still alive after this, if we win this..." Robin paused and glanced at her gloved hands, rubbing them together. "Then we go."

"When this is over..." Valerie took Robin's hands in her own. "Then, yes. If that's what you want."

They were in battle gear, gloves and all, so the gesture of taking her hands wasn't what it would have otherwise been. Still, Robin appreciated it.

"When the time comes," Robin replied.

Garcia appeared above, climbing back down. When he was most of the way he jumped, landing next to Valerie.

"No good news?" she asked

"We've cleared the tower complex," he replied, "and there's cover if we go another fifty feet before angling up. I think that would be safer."

"Makes sense," Robin said, and Valerie agreed. They pushed on, but after a few minutes a wall covered in vines shifted and everyone turned, worried and ready for an attack. The vines fell down as a small creature that resembled an armored rat darted out and ran between them.

Valerie had just let out a breath of relief when a voice said, "You found them."

All spun to see Moralu kneeling beside the strange creature with a hand on its armored back. She had five Norrul with her, all equipped with heavy club-like weapons.

Robin took a step toward them, ready for a fight, Garcia took a fighting stance. Jilla growled. However, they weren't attacking yet, and that there was doubt in the Norrul female's eyes.

"You didn't want to betray us," Valerie said. "We can let it slide...if it doesn't happen again."

Moralu stood, eyes narrowing. "We won't stand against Demus. We're not idiots."

"And if fighting us right now would result in your death?" Valerie asked. "If turning away right now could mean a possible end to Demus and his ways?"

That caused Moralu to cock her head, then sway it back and forth as the Skulla often did. "You were strong against Rokal, I'll give you that."

"You admire strength?" Valerie grinned, wondering why she hadn't put more weight into this thought before. They had their strange carapace and fights to celebrate—of course strength was what mattered. "I can show you strength. Not just me; we have Lolack's fleet—the Lost Fleet—and we have more. The Etheric Federation…you've heard of them?"

Moralu caught her breath, eyes going wide for a moment but then returning to normal as she attempted to hide the fact that she had.

"Good. We're with the Etheric Federation, as this whole system will be when Demus is destroyed."

Moralu glanced at her companions; one looked especially mean, though it was the short one behind her who gave off a strange vibe, Valerie thought. When he growled and stepped forward, she was ready for him. He raised his club and came at her, and as she side-stepped she was surprised to see Moralu catch him under the chin with her club.

Her next strike caught him across the stone protrusions on his cheek, driving them into his face, and she brought the club back around to smash them again. After the second blow, the Norrul collapsed, unconscious.

"Move," Moralu ordered. "Go to where you see three holes together and a hanging vine to the left."

"Excuse me?"

"It's a secret spot," Moralu explained, "that leads to a cave above where you'll be safe."

"Come with us," Garcia said.

"We can't," Moralu said, looking at her remaining three companions. They seemed unsure what was happening, or at least had not yet decided how they felt about it. "Our families would be in danger if we were found, or if they even suspected us of helping you."

"And when he comes to?" Valerie asked, gesturing at the male on the ground. "What do you do then?"

Moralu turned to the large Norrul. He grunted and looked at the others, then stepped forward and raised his club.

"He chose his side," the large Norrul said and brought his club down hard, slamming the stone bump in the other's cheek all the way in. Blood seeped out from the opening where it had moments ago protruded.

"Damn," Garcia said, then nodded. "And so have you all."

"Thank you," Valerie said, ignoring the now-dead Norrul at their feet. The large Norrul was right. The enemies had chosen their sides, and it was time everyone else did as well.

"Thank me by getting out of here alive and doing as you've promised. Demus cannot be allowed to continue."

"We won't let this war drag on," Valerie declared. "Trust me, it'll be over soon enough."

Moralu pointed, then turned back to her team. "No sign of them yet. Keep looking."

One of the Norrul took a moment to catch on, but the

others were already looking around, pretending to have not seen them.

Valerie, however, knew this wasn't over. "And our friends?" she asked. "The Grayhewn?"

"What do you mean?" Moralu asked.

"We lost him back there, in the tunnels."

A troubled look came over Moralu's face, and she nodded. "It's good you escaped. We'll start back, see if we can find him. However, he's likely been taken by now, either by someone with Demus's fleet or by one of our own loyal to him."

"Then we'll have to take him back," Garcia said.

Moralu smiled. "I hope you do."

With that, she joined the others who were already moving back the way they'd come.

"Well, that was...enlightening," Jilla remarked. "I didn't think their kind capable of what she just did."

"Killing one of their own?" Valerie asked.

"Taking a stance against someone like Demus."

"I think you'll find the Norrul are better allies than we would've expected," Garcia said. "The look in her eyes—that was passion. Passion like that? Not someone you want to cross."

"When it comes down to it, I'll be glad to have them on our side," Valerie said as they set off to look for the way up that Moralu had told them about.

CHAPTER THIRTEEN

PLANET RHOL

"For you to understand, you need to know a little about the Shimmers' home planet," Nostro began. They walked through the tunnels as he talked.

Since getting past the Ravagion, they had only encountered a few forks in the path. They were following the ones that angled upward now, as the Norrul female had instructed them.

"Our home planet has a name," Wearl snapped.

"Yes, sorry. It's called Uogard. The climate is not always the friendliest, and water is scarce in most regions, which makes the few areas where water is available very valuable."

Wearl explained further. "The cities are all near the water sources. We have to build upward instead of out, so most of us live in incredibly tall buildings."

Kalan listened with fascination. For some reason, he'd never thought much about the Shimmers' home planet.

Maybe it was because they were invisible, but he had never really pictured them anywhere else. In his mind, they just lived on SEDE.

He realized now how narrow-minded that was. Not every Shimmer was a prison guard, just like every Grayhewn wasn't a former prisoner.

Well, he wasn't so sure about that last part. He wasn't even sure there *were* other Grayhewns.

Nostro continued. "Oddly, there is one place where water is plentiful that the Shimmers won't go. It's an island—"

"It's not an island," Wearl interrupted. "It's a peninsula. You're messing it all up. Let me tell it."

"Fine, be my guest."

It was odd how Wearl's entire attitude toward Nostro had shifted since the fight with the Ravagion. Clearly she'd expected him to be some great monster fighter, but that he wasn't hadn't merely disappointed her. She seemed truly angry about it. Kalan was still trying to understand why, and he hoped the story the two of them were telling would shed some light on the matter.

"There used to be a city on the peninsula," Wearl continued. "It was one of our largest, and it was known for its celebration of the arts."

"Shimmers have arts?" Flynn asked.

"Of course we do. Gladiator fights. Survival competitions. Murder-swimming. All the arts."

"Murder-swimming?" Flynn asked. "Actually, never mind. I don't want to know."

"The point is, the city was a proud metropolis, until about two hundred years ago when the Borin came."

"The Borin?" Kalan asked.

"It was a huge creature, maybe three times the size of the Ravagion. It walked on its back legs, and it was covered with spiky growths. Someone called it 'Borin' and the name stuck. The biggest problems with Borin were that he appeared to be unkillable, and was constantly angry."

"That is a bad combination," Kalan admitted.

"He tore through the city, ravaging day and night. The Shimmers who lived there put up a brave fight, but they could only hold on for so long. Eventually they admitted defeat, and abandoned the city to the monster."

"Damn, that's wild," Flynn exclaimed. "I'm still not sure what any of this has to do with you getting all mad at Nostro."

"I'm getting to that. There was this seer among the Shimmer people at the time, and she made a prophecy about the Borin. She said it wouldn't reign forever—eventually a hero would arise. We would know the hero because he would pull a tooth from Borin's mouth the first time he faced him. He would be a great leader to the Shimmers for years, and in his old age he would return with an army behind him to kill the Borin once and for all."

Kalan turned to Nostro. "I take it that's where you come in? That strange blade you showed Wearl back on SEDE? She suddenly started listening to you after that."

Nostro nodded sheepishly. He pulled the strange-looking blade from his belt.

Now that Kalan knew what he was looking at, it was clear the thing was not a blade, but a tooth.

"What I want to know," Wearl snarled, "is how the hell you got your hands on that thing…if it's even real. Because based on what I saw back there, I don't believe you pulled it from the Borin's mouth."

"Oh, it's real," Nostro countered. "And I *did* pull it from the Borin's mouth. It's just that he was already dead when I did it."

There was a long pause, but finally Wearl snarled, "You're lying."

"I'm not." He thought for a moment before continuing. "When I left SEDE, I knew I wanted to find a way to help the beings on my cellblock. I figured the best way to do that was to get the Shimmers on my side, so I travelled to Uogard."

"You're lucky they didn't rip your damn head off," Wearl growled.

"Oh, a few of them tried, but I got lucky. Found someone willing to upgrade my translation chip so I could hear them, and then I heard the legend of the Borin."

"And that was when you decided to trick my people?"

"Not at all. I decided to try my hand at making the prophecy come true. Fighting has ever been my strong suit. I'm a great negotiator and I think I'm a good leader, but I'm only average in a fight. That's part of why I decided to look like this. I need all the intimidation factor I can get."

"So why'd you decide to go up against this big monster?" Flynn asked.

"I was desperate. So I travelled to the peninsula, and what I found there surprised me. I think it'll even surprise you, Wearl."

The Shimmer laughed. "If you're going to tell me the Borin was dead, you're going to have a hard time convincing me. Plenty of great warriors go to fight the

Borin, and none of them come back. If the Borin's dead, what's killing them?"

Nostro smiled sadly. "What I found was not just one Borin, but dozens. There must have been at least two of the monsters to start with, because they've been breeding. The big ugly bastards are all over that city."

There was a long pause. "That's impossible."

"Saw it with my own eyes. I also found a Borin graveyard, which was where I got the tooth." He sighed. "Look, I'm sorry I lied to you, Wearl. It was the only way I could think of to earn the respect of the guards and help my fellow prisoners."

Wearl chucked softly. "Dozens of Borin. Who'd of thought? I've always wanted to try my hand at killing that monster. Now that we know there's more than one, you can come with me Kalan and we can all kill one."

"Uh, sure, sounds like fun." Kalan turned to Nostro. "Something still doesn't add up. Wearl said great warriors go to fight the Borin all the time. How is it they don't make it back, and you did?"

Nostro smiled weakly. "Because I was a coward about it. I wasn't trying to fight the Borin. Once I realized there were many of them, I concentrated on sneaking around the city. I hid whenever they came around, and I snuck away when they left. That's how I survived."

"You are a coward," Wearl said.

Kalan wasn't so sure about that. The Pallicon had given up his freedom to help his friends and family. Nothing cowardly about that.

"You're right," Nostro admitted. "But I'd like the opportunity to change that. I want to be the hero I pretended to be."

Flynn clapped him on the back. "Well, buddy, you came to the right place. There is no shortage of opportunities for dumb displays of bravery in Valerie's Elites. You'll get your chance."

Nostro's voice was earnest when he replied, "If I do get the chance, I'm going to take it."

They continued through the tunnel for a while, always taking the upward path. After a while, Kalan spotted something in the distance. "I think that might be daylight!"

They exited the tunnel and found themselves in a landscape dominated by orange clay and strange vegetation. After walking for a few minutes, they spotted a female Norrul in the distance. She was waving at them.

"Well, she's waving rather than shooting at us," Wearl commented dryly. "We're already doing better than usual."

Flynn squinted at the Norrul. "I'm pretty sure I know her. I think that's Moralu."

They hurried toward her, and she smiled when they reached her.

"Pleased to see you," she told them. "If you're looking for Valerie, I can point you in the right direction."

Kalan and Flynn exchanged a smile. "For once, fate seems to be working in our favor."

Flynn chuckled. "Don't worry. Based on prior experience, the good luck won't last."

CHAPTER FOURTEEN

PLANET RHOL, CAVERNS

The vine hung to the left of the three holes, just as Moralu had described.

"And if we can't trust her?" Robin asked.

"We can."

Robin shrugged.

This time Valerie took the lead. She had to jump for the vine, and found that it stretched when she got a grip on it. She pulled herself up hand over hand, and soon had a view of the cavern. It had sloping walls and the strange vegetation, almost like an extension of the jungle below, but kept in an odd-shaped box.

She stood up once she'd crawled through the opening. It wasn't a cave like anything she'd seen back home, as this one was covered with a substance that rippled like water. The stone had a turquoise substance coating it. It was kind of like gelatin, and she imagined it was either alive or reacted to the vibrations of the planet.

A quick search of the immediate area showed that the Norrul had stocked this place with local nuts and water. There were several offshoots, but the cave was clear of any danger.

"Come on up," she hissed through the hole, then moved to the cave's exit, looking at the endless stretches of the clay-like ground that lay in that direction. Trying to get her bearings, she imagined the Norrul spires were behind and to her right, invisible from here. It was possible a cavern she hadn't discovered yet led that way, but she didn't have time to search. If she was in a cave at ground level, that meant there was higher ground above it. High ground meant another chance to get reach Lolack on the comm.

She realized the comm might work now, since the metal caves weren't blocking them. She tried, but got only static—no luck yet.

"What's the deal?" Robin asked, joining her at the exit.

"I'm not sure yet," Valerie replied, "but I'd imagine we can either go out and make our way up to the top, or see if there's a tunnel that leads up. We have to get that signal"

"Outside seems more likely," Robin replied. "I checked out the area inside, and didn't see much there."

The others joined them, and Valerie made the decision. "Stay here and keep a lookout. Robin and I will make a sprint for the top and try reaching Lolack, and go from there."

"And if there's no response?" Jilla asked.

"We charge back there and take down as many of those fuckers as possible," Robin replied.

"Couldn't have said it better myself," Valerie said.

"Be careful up there," Garcia said.

"Always am."

Valerie and Robin exited the cave but the first step led started to sink, so Valerie pulled back. A glance showed that the rockface of the outside looked typical—orange rocks that jutted out with lines of metal in them and small plants that grew in clumps scattered across the surface. Judging by the angle they wouldn't have a problem climbing, so that was what they did. They ascended the hill, moving along carefully, and soon were able to see past it to the tall trees beyond. They recognized those as being between them and the Norrul spires. Smoke rose in the distance from the direction of the crashed ship.

"Maybe we should've tried to find the *Grandeur*," Robin said. "Seen if we could've accessed the comm without leaving."

"And been sitting ducks when the guards—who we can't see—arrived? Or prisoners with worse things on their minds then throwing us in prison? No, thanks."

"Right, of course." Robin climbed a bit higher than Valerie and added, "But if this doesn't work, I'd say trying from the ship is our best bet."

"It could be our *only* bet," Valerie admitted.

They reached a ledge and Valerie tried the comm again. She sighed when there was no response.

Robin leaned against the rockface, staring out over the clay, and Valerie joined her. The orange light seemed to form waves; waves coming for them, then vanishing in the sky.

"What a strange planet," Robin said. "Kind of literally a shithole."

Valerie couldn't hold the laugh in. "What?"

"I mean, that stuff…it looks like shit."

"No, it doesn't." Valerie looked again, then frowned. "Damn, you're right. I was thinking clay this whole time, but yeah, shit. It looks like shit."

"Unhealthy orange shit, but shit nonetheless." Robin chuckled, then jerked a thumb at the hill. "Ready to go higher?"

Valerie nodded and led the way. Here it was less of a struggle, since the hill was now a slope that they could walk up. As they got higher the trees grew taller and denser, providing some shade.

"What do you think Kalan will do after all this?" Robin asked. "I mean, he *is* the Bandian, after all."

"Right. All those fleets flocking here because of him, in a sense." Valerie laughed. "It's funny that he feels like just another one of us, but really he could be so much more."

"So could you," Robin replied.

"What?"

"I mean, when you run around this way you're like a grunt. You should be a general, calling the shots."

"Since I'm a grunt who gets shit done, and one who can get shot and heal, I'd rather be the grunt."

Robin scoffed. "But that's what I mean. You don't think others should get hurt in the line of duty, or be allowed to risk their lives. Do you ever think that if you were in a higher position, you could do more to save lives? Making better decisions saves lives on the whole, and puts people into less worrisome situations."

"You're still annoyed that Michael put us under TH," Valerie declared.

"So what?" Robin kicked a rock and watched it tumble

partway down the hill. "And now we're under Nathan or whoever. It still doesn't make sense to me."

"Because you see me as something else," Valerie smiled, "I get that. But in the grand scheme of things, we're all part of this machine. We play our parts to keep it working."

Robin shrugged. "Where's the real enemy in all this? Point the two of us at him—or her—and I guarantee we'd end it all in no time."

"Damn, really?" Valerie shook her head, chuckling. "You think the two of us could deal with something that BA and Michael haven't?"

"Well, when you put it that way…"

"But…" Valerie looked at her friend curiously. "You did say us, didn't you? I mean, you're still seeing this as an 'us' thing?"

"Fighting the enemy always will be."

Valerie nodded, walking in silence for a bit.

"And maybe more than that," Robin added, quietly.

"What's that?"

Robin contemplated her silently for a few steps. "Nothing."

It certainly hadn't been nothing, but Valerie let it go. Curiosity took over as she wondered what Robin was thinking. Had the woman reconsidered her position on the two of them romantically? Maybe it was just the situation they found themselves in. Valerie refused to get her hopes up. There was also the possibility of not making it out of this alive.

She decided that if they did, she would push the topic. If it went nowhere, she'd dismiss it once and for all.

From the top of the hill, they could see the spires, the

crashed ship beyond, and more ships coming down from above.

"Tenowk, Lolack, anyone," Valerie said into her comm.

No answer, but no ringing or strange static either. Robin tried, but got back the same. For a moment they lingered, then Valerie tried again, but this time she kept going in case anyone was listening.

"So that's it then," Robin said, staring at the scene before them. Above were the massive ships that made up some of Demus's army. She removed her helmet. "If we're going to die…"

"Don't talk like that."

"We've survived a lot," Robin replied, gesturing into the sky, "but this?"

"Come on, I…" She stopped talking when Robin stepped over and removed her helmet too. The intensity in her eyes was too much—it stole Valerie's words, leaving her with nothing but a distant thought—one she couldn't quite grasp.

Robin leaned in and gently brought their lips together; a brush of the tongue, a lingering moment of desire and passion. She pulled away.

"Wh-what was that?" Valerie asked.

"I've been wanting to for so long," Robin replied, still unable to meet her gaze.

"But everything you've said—"

"Was true, when we're out there fighting. Not if we're possibly going to die."

Valerie considered that. Well, in that case… She stepped forward and pulled Robin close, this time making sure the kiss was one they would remember if the next hour left them dying on some alien planet. For that perfect moment, nothing else mattered. They were as one. Their passion drove them...but they were interrupted by the awkward clinking of space armor on space armor.

First to laugh was Valerie, Robin following.

"If we had more time—" Robin started.

"Right. And weren't surrounded by enemies or in a hurry to try to get back to the fleet, and save Kalan in the process."

"Yeah, all that." The woman leaned forward, cheek against Valerie's, then whispered in her ear, "We wouldn't be able to stop, would we?"

Valerie closed her eyes and breathed out as the chill ran up her spine. She licked her lips. When she opened her eyes Robin had drawn back, but there wasn't passion in her eyes anymore. It was something else—excitement mixed with relief.

"Get a good show?" Robin shouted, and Valerie spun.

There was a ship with its rear hatch open and a smiling Tenowk framed in it.

"Actually, I recorded the whole thing in my databanks," he told her with a grin. "Might broadcast it across the galaxy if you piss me off."

"Can I get a copy?" Valerie joked, earning her a punch in the arm from Robin. The punch clanged off her armor.

"Seriously, get in here!" Tenowk waved them over. "You want five minutes alone before we grab the rest of them?"

"Shut up already," Robin snapped as she ran over and jumped in, landing gracefully when he moved out of the way.

Valerie joined them a second later.

"The bad news is, we lost a couple. So...probably need to find them. Raincheck on the five minutes?"

"Val," Robin chided.

"Joking, joking." When Valerie winked at Tenowk, he held up his hand as he mouthed that she'd get her five minutes. She chuckled, wondering if she *was* joking.

"Good news, if that's what is worrying you," Tenowk said, "I saw them running this way, but figured I'd get you two first. I *was* totally joking about the five minutes, and damn...we're wasting time."

"You should probably shut-up," Valerie said, "is what I would say if you hadn't just saved our butts. Jilla, Bob, and Garcia are that way," she added, pointing.

He grinned. "Aranaught will take us right down."

Even as he said it the ship moved around to the front of the hill, where the rest were waiting. Valerie quickly explained, and they all jumped in.

"Let's go get Kalan," Valerie said, excitement rising. She realized they really might have a chance at this as the hatch closed and the ship sped off.

CHAPTER FIFTEEN

PLANET RHOL

Kalan and his friends followed Moralu's directions, walking up a nearby hill to get a vantage point. According to the Norrul, they'd be able to find Valerie and the team at a place with three holes and a vine.

"Sounds like a dirty joke," Wearl had quipped.

When they reached the top of the hill, Kalan shielded his eyes with his hand and stared north. He saw a glint on the top of another hill that could have been the light reflecting off the ship Moralu had described.

"I don't see it," he told the others.

Flynn sighed. "You know, I can't wait to get off this planet. Maybe we'll end up in a place where we have fewer enemies."

"Is there such a place?" Wearl asked.

The human grinned. "We haven't found it yet, but I remain optimistic."

Nostro sidled up beside them. "As much as I've enjoyed this brief escape, I won't be joining you when you leave."

Kalan glanced at him. "What? You going to fight the Borin for real this time?"

The big Pallicon chuckled. "No. I'm needed back at the One-Eight-Nine. I figure if I hang out near the wreckage long enough, eventually someone will show up to gather the prisoners who lived through the crash and take them back up."

Kalan shook his head. "You're crazy. I respect your commitment to Cellblock One-Eight-Nine, but you are insane."

"I'll take that as a compliment."

"You're right about one thing," a voice said behind them. "You are going back SEDE. Every damn one of you."

Kalan recognized the voice, and his hand started toward his gun.

"Don't even think about it," Captain Tuttle said. "Hands in the air. Turn around slowly."

Kalan did as he was told, as did the others.

Captain Tuttle stood there grinning at them with his pistol raised. Ten prisoners stood behind him, many of them battered and bloodied from the crash.

"I see you've been rounding up prisoners," Kalan said.

Tuttle nodded. "With a little help from the Shimmers. These ten agreed to help me hunt the rest in exchange for a slight reduction in their sentences."

Kalan looked the prisoners over. He couldn't help but feel sorry for them, even though they were working with Tuttle. They hadn't asked for any of this, and were just doing the best they could with what had happened to them.

"Let's head back to the crash site," Tuttle said. "We'll wait there for the transport back to SEDE, where all of you will be spending the rest of your natural lives."

Flynn frowned. "Um, you know I'm not a SEDE prisoner, right?"

"You are now. You made a poor choice in friends. Let's move."

A loud *crack* split the air, and Tuttle's head rocked back as if he'd been punched.

"Let's not," Wearl said, plucking the gun from his hand. "People always forget about Shimmers, but I didn't think the captain of SEDE would."

Tuttle staggered, trying to keep his footing. With a furious scowl on his tattooed face, he turned to the prisoners. "Anyone who kills one of these bastards walks out of SEDE free and clear."

The prisoners looked at each other for a moment in surprise, then turned their gazes on Kalan, Nostro, and Flynn.

"Uh, this doesn't seem good," Flynn said with a scared hitch in his voice.

Kalan's hand went to his pistol again but he hesitated, then decided not to draw the weapon. He couldn't shoot these prisoners—not unless he absolutely had to. Instead, he raised his fists and set his feet. He glanced at Flynn and Nostro. "Don't hurt them more than you have to."

"Does that include me?" Wearl asked.

"Of course!"

The prisoners charged.

Kalan immediately homed in on the biggest of them, a genetically-modified Skulla with massive shoulders and arms to match. The guy looked incredibly strong, but he wasn't too steady on his feet—a product of his unnatural musculature. Kalan stood his ground as the Skulla charged, but at the last moment he dodged left and drove his fist into the prisoner's stomach.

The force of Kalan's punch combined with the momentum of the running Skulla to produce a devastating impact. The Skulla doubled over and fell to the ground.

He saw a Pallicon slam a fist into Flynn's jaw, and the human staggered backward.

Kalan let out an involuntary growl of anger and charged. He delivered a massive uppercut to the Pallicon, and his fist connected with the underside of the male's jaw. Somehow, the prisoner remained on his feet, and he punched Kalan in the ribs.

"Are you sure I can't kill these guys?" Wearl asked.

"What? No?" Kalan tried to stay focused on his opponent, who once again hit him in the side.

"Just one?"

"Wearl, I'm a little busy. Don't kill anyone!" Kalan dropped his elbow to catch the Pallicon's next punch on the arm instead of his battered ribs, then responded with a powerful jab that cracked the prisoner's nose.

He took a quick look around to see how his friends were doing. Nostro was fighting a second genetically-modified Skulla, and he appeared to be making his way to Captain Tuttle. Flynn had taken on a lanky Skulla, and though the human was bigger, the Skulla was fast as hell and was putting up a respectable fight.

"Last chance, Kalan."

He turned and saw Captain Tuttle. Somehow he'd gotten his gun back, and he had it trained on Kalan. "Tell your friends to stand down, or I will shoot you. I'd prefer not to—Grayhewns are an endangered species, after all. But I'll do it if I have to."

Kalan gritted his teeth. There was no way he was going back to SEDE, not after everything he'd done to get out. And he certainly wasn't going to let this idiot capture Flynn or Wearl.

"Kalan, you need to get out of here," Nostro called. He'd dropped the Skulla he'd been fighting and was stalking toward the captain.

"What are you doing, Nostro?" Kalan shouted.

"Just a dumb display of bravery." With that, he sprinted toward the captain.

Tuttle had just enough time to turn before Nostro slammed into him. The Skulla captain's small body lifted right off the ground when the big Pallicon hit him. Nostro's momentum carried them off the top of the hill and they tumbled down the side, still locked in combat.

"Damn," Flynn said. "That was dumb."

Kalan grabbed his arm. "Nostro bought us a little time, so let's make good use of it." He turned to the prisoners. "You shouldn't be fighting us. You want freedom? Don't wait for Captain Tuttle to give it to you. I don't see any chains on your hands. You're already free."

The prisoners just stared at him. It wasn't clear whether they'd taken his words to heart, but at least they weren't attacking anymore.

Kalan trotted down the hill, heading toward the location where they hoped to find Valerie.

They'd only started down the hill when a glint of light appeared in the distance. A ship approaching. Kalan tensed, wondering if it had been spotted.

The ship landed not far in front of them. The door opened and someone climbed out. Valerie!

Kalan smiled when he saw his friend, but he felt a little sadness at what had just transpired too. He felt odd leaving Nostro behind—like he should go back and fight to save his new friend—but the Pallicon had made his intentions clear. He wanted to return to SEDE, and he'd attacked the captain to give Kalan and the others time to get away. Going back now would be disrespecting Nostro's wishes.

When they reached the ship, they were delighted to see Valerie and the others gathered around it. Kalan greeted her with a hug.

Valerie grinned. "Took you long enough to get out of the tunnels."

"Yeah, well, we had a complication or two on the way."

"Us too," Valerie replied.

Bob walked up to Flynn and gave him a nod. "So you're with Kalan on his missions now?"

Flynn laughed. "It wasn't exactly my choice. Kinda just happened. Wait, are you jealous?"

Bob's face reddened. "What? No, of course not."

Jilla put a hand on Bob's shoulder. "I got left out too. Don't feel bad."

Kalan chuckled. "I would have loved to have had both of you along, especially when we fought the monster."

"There was a monster?" Now the jealousy was clear in Bob's voice.

"Just small one," Flynn explained. "Well, small*ish*. Big teeth, though."

Valerie nudged Kalan. "Hey, you haven't met Tenowk yet, have you?"

She led him onto the ship, and the others followed. They found someone working on the wiring near the bridge.

"Tenowk, meet Kalan."

Tenowk started to turn, but he suddenly froze. "No. Not now."

Concern furrowed Valerie's brow. "Are you okay?"

Tenowk frantically began inspecting the panel next to the wires. "No! He's getting into the ship! And into my head! The enemy is here!"

CHAPTER SIXTEEN

PLANET RHOL, TENOWK'S SHIP

Tenowk was pulling out wires and connecting them to the metal in his head, shouting about pain and crazy things, too.

"Dragons all around me! I can't stop them!" he yelled, then turned to Valerie with white eyes. "Plug in. I can't do it alone."

"Plug—what?" she asked, but he was holding out his hands, cables connected to his gloves, and she had a damn good idea what he meant. She hated the idea, but knew she needed this guy to get them out of there. If he needed help and said this was the way to do it, she'd step up.

As soon as she was close enough, he placed his hands on her exposed head and she felt pulses of electricity go through her. For a moment, she wondered if she'd made a terrible mistake. This could be the end of her, if the electricity fried her beyond healing.

Well, at least she'd had that kiss. With a smile she

focused on that—and then felt her eyes roll back into her head as visions hit her.

Tenowk was shouting at her as she stood in front of him, only they weren't on the ship anymore. They were on a planet with purple gasses floating around them like fog.

A roaring dragon appeared through the gasses, coming for them.

"It's not real," Tenowk told her. "Neither are we."

"Then what do we do?" she asked, voice rising in panic when the dragon opened its mouth. Purple light glowed in its throat.

"Fight as if it were real, but remember that it's not—and that rules can be broken."

She blinked and was about to say something when Tenowk shouted, "Dive!" and took her down with him as the dragon shot a blast of plasma at them. It ate up the ground where they'd stood a moment before...and the attack kept coming.

Tenowk pulled Valerie up and they ran. He explained, "Demus hacked into our system and is in my mind, or Aranaught's."

"All of this is just him fucking with us?"

"You got it."

They dove again, then Valerie got up, ready to attack. "What if I kill the dragon?"

"It's just something he conjured up, so it won't matter," Tenowk replied as the dragon circled back into the gasses, likely preparing for another strike.

"So?" She held out her hands, desperate. "Tell me what to do!"

"You need to distract him to the same extent he's

distracting me," Tenowk responded. "Then I'll be able to hack him back and break the connection so we can get off Rhol and reconnect with Lolack's fleet."

"Done. How?"

He pointed, and she saw it—the ship she'd seen Demus arrive on earlier, when they were near the Silahu ruins.

"So if it's not real, can I jump all that way?" she asked.

"If you accept that, and really *believe* it," he replied. "Like that movie...what was it?"

"Probably didn't see it, remember?" she said. "Here goes!"

She took a running start and leaped, going all-out. She drew an imaginary sword as she flew. The jump had to have been over two hundred feet, but she was about to land on the ship when the dragon slammed into her.

They spun past the gasses into space. She held on with one hand as she slashed at its scales with her sword. They were too tough! Or they would have been, if this were real. Remembering that it wasn't, she focused on her next action producing the result she wanted. She changed the sword into a bridle and threw it around the dragon's snout.

She had it, and with a quick tug turned the beast for the ship. The dragon barreled toward Demus, and she saw him on the bridge, staring at her with his wild helmet. He braced as the dragon slammed into the ship.

She leaped from the dragon onto the ship and ran to the hatch. Each punch and kick dented the material, and the damage got worse as she focused on the false nature of this place.

"Keep it up," Tenowk said, his voice louder as he increased in size. Electricity crackled from his hands, and he shot in all directions. For a moment the place lit up, and what had appeared to be deep space surrounding them was revealed to be wires and more cables, as if they were inside the ship—or maybe even a computer of sorts.

For a moment she was back at the ship, Tenowk's hands still on her head. Robin and Bob were looking at them like they were crazy. She screamed as more electricity hit her and she was gone again; back on that space ship, only now it was transforming and sending flames of metal out to capture her legs and arms.

She shouted for strength and pulled against the metal, and with a massive jerk that cramped all her muscles, she pulled the metal free of the ship. The ship shuddered, then began to fall. The metal still clung to her arms and legs so she shook it off, saw the purple gasses and the planet approaching, and timed her jump.

She crashed to the ground and turned to see Tenowk standing over her, still shooting out electricity, while Demus charged out of his crashed ship.

He glared at her, then at the large form of Tenowk.

"You two are cowards!" he spat. "Why resist when we can unite and work together for the universe's greater good!"

"When a plan involves slavery and mass murder, it's not for the greater good," Valerie replied. "No matter what the goal."

He growled and charged her, his army of robots appearing behind her, and then she charged him.

"*Now!*" Tenowk shouted and the electricity exploded... and then Valerie was back at their ship. Tenowk stumbled to the bridge and collapsed into the pilot seat, saying, "Strap in, ladies and gents. It's go time."

With that the ship—the real ship, outside of that crazy experience—shuddered and shot into the air.

"I've taken over," Aranaught's voice said. Tenowk just nodded, as if she were present and could see him.

Valerie turned to Robin, who ran over and caught her in her arms as she nearly collapsed.

"Here, sit, sit," Robin insisted, guiding her to the seat next to Tenowk's. "What the hell happened just now?"

Valerie grinned. "You wouldn't believe me if I told you."

"Fine, just get us out of here and I'll be as happy as they come."

A glance at the display showed enemies in pursuit, but then the image changed and Admiral Lolack appeared.

"You got them, Tenowk?"

Tenowk mumbled and gestured to Valerie.

"We're here, Admiral," Valerie said. "Ran into some trouble, but we're back on course and we have..." She held up the orb, which they'd obtained from the prison ship.

"I don't suppose it came with an instruction manual?" Lolack asked.

"No?"

"It's just, the last being who truly know how to operate it died," Lolack admitted.

Valerie's mouth dropped open and her rage started to work its way up, beginning with her legs shaking slowly. *"Then why exactly were we after it?"*

"I'd thought I could find a way, but it's proving futile. Damn, if only Sslake were still alive—"

"Sslake, Admiral?" Kalan interjected, stepping in from the back. "He is."

"What?" Lolack exclaimed. "No, he—"

"It's true," Valerie chimed in. "You'll see him once we land on Tol. We sort of rescued him from SEDE, then put him in power over Tol. A joint project, you could say."

Kalan beamed at her, and Lolack stared, impressed.

"You heard her," he shouted to his crew. "All hands, we're going to Tol for our final defense!"

"And we'll need an escort, sir," Tenowk managed to get out.

"Right. My best three ships, see that Tenowk and the others get here safely."

There were shouts of confirmation, and then Tenowk turned back to Valerie and crew and grinned. "Time to test you."

As shots kept coming and ships fell in behind them to join in the chase, Valerie leaned back and closed her eyes. This was going to be a long flight, and there wasn't much else she could do at the moment.

CHAPTER SEVENTEEN

PLANET TOL

When the ship finally touched down on Tol, Kalan was so relieved that he could have kissed the ground.

The entire flight had been a battle, with Demus's ships constantly harassing them. Never swarming them or making an all-out assault, but also never giving them a moment's reprieve.

Kalan had manned one of the railguns, and he'd spent hours discouraging the fighters with directed fire. What made it even more frustrating was that in all that time, he wasn't sure he'd taken out even one of the bastards.

Bob stepped off the ship and slapped Kalan's back. "Well, buddy, that was utterly exhausting. Thank God they had us along though, right? The way we handle our guns? You just don't find that every day."

"No one wants to hear about the way you handle your gun, Bob," Jilla interjected. "Besides, I think the Lavkins had a little something to do with our survival, too."

Kalan grinned. Even though he hadn't officially reunited with his new family yet, it felt good to hear Lien and Mej's voices over the comm. They were both aboard *Flamebird*, Lien's family ship, which had been one of the three sent to help protect their ship.

And as Jilla had said, the members of the formerly Lost Fleet had proven to be just as good as their reputation, and had kept Demus's ships from doing any real damage.

Kalan took a look around. Now that his feet were on solid ground, it was time to get back to business. He hadn't been on Tol much since Sslake took over leadership from the false Bandian. From what Valerie and the others had said there were real changes to the lives of many of the residents, even if they weren't obvious from a single glance.

He chuckled at the irony of it all. Here they were, back where everything had begun. Well, technically it had begun on a transport ship not far from this planet, but this was where he'd really started working with Valerie and her Elites.

Kalan briefly wondered what his life would be like now if he'd just kept his seat on that transport when the Pallicon hijackers came aboard. Valerie and her team probably would have saved everyone anyway.

But he never would have joined them. He would never have met Wearl or reunited with Jilla, or even learned the truth about his people. Most likely he'd be a transport pilot, bored out of his skull.

His life would be simpler, but it would have far less meaning.

As Valerie and the others exited the vessel, a group of armed Skulla approached.

The one in front stepped up to Valerie. Clearly he'd seen the Prime Enforcer before, and knew she was in charge. "Sslake would like to see you as soon as possible."

Valerie frowned. "Right to business, huh? Probably a good idea, what with the enemy fleet on its way here to kill us all."

The Skulla guards went pale.

Robin leaned forward. "She's joking. I mean, not about the enemy fleet, but the killing-us-all thing. Well, now that I think about it, they *are* trying to kill us all. But we won't let them. I'll be quiet now."

From the looks on the guards' faces, it was clear they found her words anything but comforting.

Valerie shook her head. "Let's just go."

Ten minutes later Valerie, Robin, and Kalan were sitting in a room with a strange oblong table. The others had remained with the ship.

They waited only a few minutes before Sslake walked in, followed closely by Admiral Lolack.

Valerie raised an eyebrow in surprise. "Wow, glad to see you two have met. Didn't wait for us to get started?"

Lolack rubbed his orange chin with his willowy fingers. "There was no time. Demus's fleet grows closer by the moment." He nodded toward Kalan. "A warm reunion to you, brother."

Kalan nodded back awkwardly. "Same to you, Admiral. Brother. Brother Admiral?" He suddenly wished he'd spent more time learning the Lavkins' customs. There was probably some official response he was supposed to be making right now. This was his first time meeting Lolack. The Shimmers had hauled Kalan away before the admiral had returned from his exile. It warmed Kalan that this important Lavkin greeted him like family.

Sslake took his place at the head of the oblong table and gave Valerie a long, hard look. "Am I really just supposed to take your word for it that a fleet is coming to attack us? What if this is all a ruse to get me to reveal my defensive protocol?"

"Uh, excuse me?" Valerie asked.

Sslake nodded grimly. "For all I know, you've decided someone else should rule and you're planning to overthrow me like you overthrew the false Bandian."

Valerie started to rise, but Robin was already on her feet.

"Overthrow you? After everything Valerie's done for you, you would dare to—"

She stopped speaking when she realized Sslake was laughing.

"I'm sorry, I couldn't help myself," Sslake said, barely getting the words out between fits of laughter. "It's so rare I get to screw with someone like that. I always have to be so official."

Kalan frowned. "There are less dangerous people to screw with. Besides, is this really the time for pranks? We're sort of on the clock here."

Sslake struggled to control his laughter. "I take my fun where I can. This job is actually quite boring." He took a deep breath, finally suppressing his chortles. "In all seriousness, thank you all for coming to my rescue. Again."

"We haven't rescued anyone yet," Valerie pointed out.

"But we're damn sure going to try. Maybe this will help." She reached into her bag and pulled out the orb. "We're not sure exactly how it works, but apparently it's a big deal. Some sort of ultimate protection?"

Sslake took the orb from her and examined it closely. "This is incredible. I think I might know what this is. Maybe not exactly what it does, but how to use it." He pressed a button embedded in the table and continued speaking. "The false Bandian did quite a bit of experimentation in his brief reign."

"We remember," Kalan said, thinking of the cyborg he'd encountered on Tol's moon.

"Not just of the AI or cybernetic variety either. We have reason to believe he was communicating with someone off-planet to acquire new ways to use ancient technologies. This orb might be one of the things he developed to work with this old tech."

"What makes you say that?" Lolack asked.

Sslake smiled. "Because there's an odd machine hard-wired into this building, and it has an orb-shaped indentation in the control panel. There are similar machines across the planet. So far, we've been unable to determine their purpose. What if the programming for the machine is contained in this orb?"

As he finished speaking, a female Skulla entered. She marched to Sslake and stood ramrod straight. "You called, sir?"

He held out the orb. "Yes. I want you to put this orb in the Bandian's machine."

She nodded crisply and took it.

"Hold up," Valerie said. "Is this a good idea? You admitted you don't really know what this thing does."

Sslake glanced at Lolack. "How long until the enemy fleet arrives?"

Lolack shook his head. "Difficult to tell. Their strange ships are messing with our sensors. Could be any moment."

"Then there's no time to waste." Sslake turned back to Valerie. "We know this is the ultimate protection, and we know the Bandian built it into this building, which was his home at the time. He was crazy, but he wasn't suicidal. Admittedly it's a risk, but it's one we have to take."

Valerie frowned. "Your call. You're the boss of this planet."

"Thanks to you." Sslake looked at the female Skulla. "Tell me when you activate it."

"Yes, sir." She marched out of the room.

"Well, here we go." Kalan grinned. "Into the unknown once again."

Sslake nodded. "It won't be as much fun as escaping SEDE with you was. I wish I could relive that. Gods, that was fun!"

Kalan couldn't help but chuckle at the wistful look in the leader's eyes. "If I remember correctly, we were running for our lives."

Valerie leaned forward. "Speaking of excitement, there's something you should know. We have reason to believe Demus is targeting leaders. He wants to hold them personally responsible for any injustice on their planet."

Sslake's face darkened. "I see."

"I'm not trying to freak you out, but you deserve to

know the truth. If we lose this fight, things could go very badly for you."

He smiled weakly. "Then we'd better not lose."

"My thoughts exactly," Valerie confirmed.

Just then, Lolack's communicator beeped. Mej's voice came through loudly enough for everyone in the room to hear it.

"Heads up, brother. We have our first confirmed eyes-on sighting of the enemy fleet. They're starting to breach the atmosphere, and there's a hell of a lot more of them coming."

"We could really use that ultimate protection thing about now," Robin pointed out.

Lolack touched the communicator. "Thank you, sister. Have the fleet engage. Do what you can to keep them out of the atmosphere as long as possible."

"You got it. *Flamebird* out."

They waited in tense silence for what would happen next. They could be boarding their ship and preparing for an aerial fight, but until they knew what the orb did they were better off biding their time.

Kalan glanced at Valerie, who was nervously tapping her foot on the floor. This was the toughest part of any battle for her, he knew...the waiting. The part where she had no control over the outcome. She was designed for action, not waiting.

That was part of what he loved about her. She didn't seem to get caught up in her own head the way he sometimes did. She knew what was right and what was wrong, and she quickly leaped into action to fight for justice—real justice—whenever possible.

After what felt like forever, a voice emerged from the speaker built into the table. "Sir, we're ready to activate the machine."

"Go ahead," Sslake quickly directed.

"Activating now."

For a long moment it seemed that nothing had happened, then something outside the large window caught Kalan's attention. It took him five seconds of staring to figure out what had changed, but once he realized it his mouth fell open.

The sky had changed color. It was now a pale, dirty brown.

Lolack's comm beeped again.

"Lolack, something really odd is happening," Mej relayed.

The admiral was staring out the window so intently he almost forgot to answer. "Yes, we can see that. Are you scanning it?"

"Yes, getting a reading. One second... Okay, damn. It's a shield—the most powerful one I've ever seen. There's no way we could pierce this thing with a fleet's worth of ammo."

"A shield?" Sslake asked. "Where?"

Mej's answer was immediate. "Everywhere. It's around the whole damn planet!"

Kalan's eyes widened. The ultimate protection. Of course. A planetary shield.

"This is incredible," Sslake exclaimed. "We're saved."

"I'm not so sure," Mej replied. "We've got a problem. Most of the enemy fleet is still in space atmosphere, but a good number of them got into the atmosphere. Maybe thirty ships, including what looks like their flagship."

Lolack's orange brow furrowed. "Thirty ships should be no problem for the Lavkin fleet. Take them down, sister."

There was a long pause. "Yeah, that's sort of the problem. Most of our ships were outside the atmosphere too. We've got ten."

Kalan's skin went cold. Ten ships versus thirty. The Lavkin fleet was the best in the world, but was it good enough to beat those odds?

"Some of the ships are going to get through," Valerie said.

Lolack nodded reluctantly. "We'll do our best, but I doubt we'll be able to stop them all from landing."

Valerie looked at Robin. "We need to prepare to fight them when they land."

"Good news is, we know where they're headed," Robin pointed out. "If Demus is after the leader, he'll come here."

"And we'll be waiting to stop him." Valerie looked at Kalan. "How about you? You going to join me and Robin on the ground, or join Lolack in the sky?"

He thought about that, considering where he could do the most good. He hated the idea of waiting on the ground when his piloting skills could come in handy in the sky, but it wasn't like he could do much piloting on the big Lavkin ships.

Lolack's comm beeped and Mej's voice came through again. "Hey, brother, one more small ship made it through before the shield went up. He's almost to the palace. Claims to be a friend of Kalan's."

Kalan tilted his head, wondering who that could

possibly be. Just about every friend he had was already on Tol, or above it.

"Says his name's Nostro. Also, he brought a gift for Kalan. Something from back home, he says. A Nim, whatever the hell that is."

A smile appeared on Kalan's face. "Oh, hell yeah! I guess that answers that question. I'm hitting the skies. Tell Nostro I'm driving."

Valerie started to stand, but Sslake stopped her.

"Wait. I have something to say first. The things you three have already done for me... I don't know how to thank you. And now you're putting your lives on the line for me again." Tears stood in the leader's eyes as he spoke. "I want you to know that whatever happens here today, you've changed Tol. You've changed this system. You've changed *me*."

Kalan swallowed hard, pushing down the lump in his throat. Sslake's words made him want to fight even harder for this leader and his planet.

"When this is over, can we count on you to support the Etheric Federation?" Valerie asked.

"You have my word," Sslake replied with a salute—both fists to his chest.

Valerie nodded, clearly touched. "We're not going to let you down, Sslake. Demus dares say he fights for justice, when all he really wants is control. He's come to the wrong planet today. It's time for us to show that metallic asshole what justice is all about."

CHAPTER EIGHTEEN

PLANET TOL

Already the attackers were coming, and not just in the air. Well, they were coming from the air, but exiting their ships before coming in hard for the fight. Some of the enemy ships that had entered before the planetary shield went up had opened their doors, and enemies were already pouring out.

"What are they thinking?" Garcia asked, shocked by the gray forms plummeting toward Tol.

"They're as eager to get to the fight as I am," Valerie replied, gripping her rifle and wishing she still had her sword.

"But this..." Robin began, staring up, dumbfounded.

"Watch!"

As they fell, it became clear that this hodgepodge of Norrul and other alien races wore thick space armor complete with space-diving gear. They came down hard, but before reaching the ground they spread out. Thrusters in the arms helped to slow them, the job completed by small tactical chutes that they cut off as soon as they hit.

Sslake's army began peppering the sky with bullets and anti-aircraft missiles, but enough were already on the ground to do damage—and then the ships began firing back.

"Remember, no matter what happens, I love you guys," Garcia called.

"Shut up. You're not going to get hurt in this," Flynn replied.

"Not me, of course. I meant you folks. I'm good."

"That a challenge?"

Garcia grinned. "All the best fights involve a kill-count contest, right?"

"Only when you're crazy," Valerie interjected, eyeing them. "In this case, yeah, that fits."

Flynn laughed and Garcia joined him.

"Let's clear them out," Robin said, already starting to jog toward the fight, rifle at her shoulder.

"You heard her," Valerie added, and charged forward at her friend's side. After what had happened back on the hilltop on Rhol she wasn't quite sure if "friend" was the right term anymore, but until they were out of this mess it certainly didn't matter.

"We've got help," Robin shouted excitedly. Sure enough, some of Aranaught's mechs had apparently made it through, because they were plowing through groups of the space-diving enemy. Others hovered and unloaded with railguns and shoulder cannons.

"They're taking away my points!" Garcia protested, then

darted forward as fast as he could, already shooting into the troops in the sky.

"One hundred and fifty," Aranaught's voice rang from the closest mech, which turned to look at Garcia. "What's your count?"

"Shut up," he replied, shooting an enemy out of the sky. "Shut up, plus one."

"Do try to keep up," Aranaught encouraged, then surged forward as the mech pulled up a plasma shield that absorbed the first two blasts from a ship still well over-head. The third connected, though, blowing off the mech's head.

Another took its place and flew toward the ship.

Four of the space divers swept in, one with blades drawn. It tried to charge right through Valerie but she dodged under and caught it by the ankle, slamming it to the ground and then spinning and unleashing a kick so that it flew up and took down two of its comrades.

She engaged in combat with two more, diving behind a berm for cover as they shot explosive rounds at her and her comrades. An explosion hit the berm as Robin leaped over and part of her armor broke off as she landed with her backside smoking.

"Dammit, watch your ass!" Valerie yelled.

"I thought that was your job," Robin replied and then was up again and shooting back at them.

Had Robin been flirting in the middle of combat? Maybe the woman was starting to get a little *too* into this, Valerie thought. She chuckled and followed suit, but after ducking back down a third time she glanced up. Now she saw why the ships weren't coming in low yet. They were focused on Tol's fleet, which had yet to take off.

Kalan was among them.

"Come on, Kalan," Valerie mumbled as she grabbed an attacker by the faceplate and slammed her into the ground, then came up to send several rounds into another attacker that was about to land a blow on Robin.

"Thanks!" Robin shouted, but Valerie was already moving on to take down the next one. She was too distracted for anything else, eyes darting to the sky periodically as she worried that Kalan and the others wouldn't make it out in time.

CHAPTER NINETEEN

PLANET TOL

Kalan stretched out in the pilot's seat of the Nim fighter. "Ah, it feels so good to be back in the cockpit."

There was a long moment of silence, then Bob looked at the apparently empty seat Wearl occupied. "Seriously? You're going to let a comment about his cockpit feeling good go without saying anything?"

Wearl sighed. "Some of us have matured since last time we flew together."

"Really?"

"No. I was just deciding between five different responses."

Bob grinned. "It *is* pretty great to be together again, isn't it?"

Nostro reached over and clapped him on the shoulder. "Indeed it is."

Bob leaned close to Kalan. "Who's this guy again?"

"I'll tell you the whole story later." Kalan shook his head

and smiled. In truth, it *did* feel pretty good to have Bob back with the group. Jilla was still on the ground since her fighting skills could come in handy there, but Valerie had figured Bob would be of more use in the sky. Wearl had simply refused to leave Kalan's side during the battle.

Mej's voice came through the radio. "Kalan, you airborne?"

"Indeed I am, sister." The word sounded odd coming out of his mouth, but now that he was part of the Lavkin family, he'd better start addressing them according to their customs.

"Good. We need you to stay low. If any of Demus's ships slip past us, you need to blow them out of the sky."

"It would be my pleasure."

"All right, we'll be in radio contact. Stay safe."

With that, she signed off.

Kalan scanned the monitors in front of him. He knew the enemy fleet had strange ships that somehow avoided detection, so he was going to have to use his eyes as well as his equipment. For now, though, the brownish skies around them appeared to be clear.

"So, Nostro, how the hell did you get your hands on a Nim fighter?"

The Pallicon grinned. "It sort of fell into my lap. There were a few docked in a secret hangar in the part of the ship that crashed. Apparently Tuttle used them for his unofficial missions."

"Speaking of Tuttle..." Kalan prompted.

"He won't be bothering anyone anymore." His voice was firm and full of conviction.

"Good." Kalan only hoped that whoever they got to

replace Tuttle would make the conditions a bit better for the SEDE prisoners, including his mother. He'd have a word with Sslake about that after the battle—assuming he survived.

"Kalan," Bob called, pointing outside the cockpit.

Kalan looked to where the human was pointing and saw a small dot on the horizon. He engaged the throttle and sent the Nim flying toward the enemy ship. "Good eye, Bob."

Bob touched the radio. "Mej, we're after one that slipped through."

"Blast it all!" she responded. "We didn't see it. Let's hope we didn't miss any others."

As they reached the enemy ship, Kalan saw it was a midsized vessel; definitely not a fighter. It had a strange boxy shape, and an odd rectangular device was attached to the bottom. An orange stripe ran along the top.

Kalan wondered how many of the metal-equipped Norrul that ship could carry...and how many residents of Tol would die if he let it get through. No way was that happening.

He banked hard to the left to put the transport directly in front of them and fired. The railgun spat, and smoke rose from the front of the transport.

"Direct hit!" Nostro shouted. "Well done."

"That's how we do it!" Bob exclaimed.

Kalan took a long look at the transport, confirming that the damage he'd inflicted would make it inoperable. With any luck, the ship would crash so far from the capital that any passengers who survived wouldn't make it to the battle until it had been over for a week.

Mej's voice came through the comm again. "Kalan, another one got through. Head northwest. You should be able to pick this one up on your scanners."

"Another transport?" he asked.

"No, this one's a fighter."

Kalan gritted his teeth as he angled the Nim to the northwest.

"I love watching you in a fight," Wearl gushed. "You get so intense. It's hot."

"It really is," Bob agreed. "I mean, from a platonic perspective."

Kalan did his best to ignore the conversation.

A few moments later, Nostro pointed at the monitor screen. "There!"

Sure enough, a blip indicated an aircraft a little to the north.

"Apparently they don't shield their fighters as well as their transports," Bob noted.

Kalan nodded. "Yeah. Let's make them pay for that mistake."

The fighter spotted them just as easily as they'd spotted it. The enemy fired, and Kalan had to pivot hard to avoid the attack.

"Well, their guns are bigger than ours," Nostro commented.

"But they're slow." Kalan dove, then brought them back up. "This one's yours, Bob."

Bob gripped the co-pilot's controls and fired. "Got 'em!"

The fighter spun wildly out of control, the direct hit disabling it.

"Nice!" Kalan exclaimed. As he was speaking, something

caught his eye. A transport, heading directly for the capitol. It had an orange stripe running down the top, and for a moment Kalan figured that must be how they painted all their transports. Then he took a closer look.

"Am I crazy, or is that the ship we shot down?" Wearl asked.

"You're not crazy." Kalan could clearly see the damage he'd inflicted on the hull. Strangely, the damage seemed less bad than it had five minutes ago. As he got closer, the hole in the hull seemed to be closing.

He activated the comm.

"Mej, this is going to sound crazy, but I think these ships can repair themselves midflight."

It took her a long moment to answer. "Damn it, brother, that does sound crazy, but I think you're right. We just thought the ships could take a beating, but you're onto something."

"We have to keep shooting even after we think we've downed them."

"Agreed. Thanks for the heads-up."

The transport was nearly at the capitol now. Kalan fired, but the transport did a surprisingly smooth roll and avoided the attack.

"How can something so ugly fly so well?" Bob asked with awe.

Kalan slammed his hand against the controls in frustration. The transport was almost on the ground now. How many would die because he hadn't taken care of business?

"Mej, I let one get through. I'm thinking about doing something very stupid."

The transport touched down, and a dozen metallic Norruls poured out the instant it hit the ground.

"Do it, Kalan," Mej replied. "We've got things under control. These ships are tough, but their pilots are not Lavkins."

"Roger that." Kalan turned toward the others. "Ready to get our hands dirty?"

"Oh, thank Borin," Wearl exclaimed. "It's been too long since I've killed anything."

Kalan took one last look at the transport. The Norruls were too spread out for him to take them out from the air, and they were moving quickly toward the capitol. "Now would be a super time to doublecheck your safety harness."

With that, he set them down in the road. Speed was his only concern for the landing, and he felt every bone in his body jar with the impact.

After visually confirming everyone was all right, he unhooked his harness and took off his helmet. "Let's go kill some bad guys."

A moment later, he burst out of the Nim and onto a street of the Tol capitol. For a moment he was disoriented, but then he spotted them.

Twelve furious Norruls with metallic carapaces rushed at them, weapons drawn.

Kalan didn't wait to see if the others were keeping up. He raced toward the closest Norrul, his Tralen-14 in his hand. The creature snarled when it saw Kalan and raised its weapon, but Kalan was faster. He fired, catching the ugly creature in the face. It let out a tremendous howl as it fell.

Kalan rushed over and put two more rounds in its

throat above the carapace to make sure it stayed down.

By the time Kalan looked up, the rest of the team was in action. Bob had brought his big rifle, and he fired at a Norrul with battle fury on his face. Nostro apparently preferred to work in close. He rushed one of the metallic Norruls and shoved his weapon into the creature's face before firing.

Even though Kalan couldn't see Wearl, he could see her impact. A Norrul was knocked over, apparently by nothing. Before it could recover from its surprise, it had a bullet through its head.

Still, the team was only doing well because most of the Norruls weren't focusing on them. They were trying to get past them to the capitol building.

Kalan shouted to the team, "Let's keep them contained! Don't let them get past you!"

Bob looked at him dumbly while a Norrul ran right past him, but thankfully Wearl was on the case, and the being fell to her invisible attack.

Another Norrul raced toward Kalan.

"Out of the way, prison scum," it shouted as it ran.

Kalan smiled. "You're really going to wish you hadn't said that." He set his feet and lunged forward as the Norrul reached him.

His shoulder slammed into the metal carapace. It didn't feel great and he felt something give in his shoulder, but the Grayhewn succeeded in knocking the Norrul back. The creature grabbed Kalan's gun hand, so Kalan drew back his empty left hand and punched him as hard as he could in the face.

The Norrul staggered backward, and Kalan raised his

pistol and fired.

As his enemy fell, Kalan turned and saw a Norrul about fifteen feet away wrestling with something invisible. Wearl.

Another Norrul was approaching from behind with a long barbed spear in its hand.

"No!" Kalan shouted. He sprinted toward the spear-wielding Norrul and threw himself at him just before the tip reached Wearl.

The Norrul spun, bringing his spear around. Kalan felt something tear at his face and realized one of the barbs had caught him. He let out an involuntary shout, then pushed the pain away and grabbed the spear, wrestling it away from him with one hand. He raised the gun in his other hand and fired.

Then he turned, pressed his weapon against the Norrul wrestling with Wearl, and fired again.

"Thanks, but I could have handled it," Wearl told him.

Kalan wiped his face with the back of his hand, and it came away bloody. "Maybe so, but we're family, remember? We help each other out."

"Kalan, you're hurt." There was a hint of panic in her voice.

"I'm fine." But even as he said the words, he wasn't sure if they were true. The entire right side of his face felt like it was on fire and blood was pouring into his right eye, blinding him. Or was the blood coming *from* his eye?

He didn't want to think about it now. There would be time for that after the fight.

Looking around, he saw that they'd taken out all the Norruls who'd exited the transport.

"Nice work, team. Let's get to the capitol building. I think we can do more good on the ground at this point."

The four of them trotted toward the capitol. It didn't take long for them to reach it, and when they did they saw that their help was indeed needed.

Norruls and Skulla were engaged in battle all around them.

"I guess a few more transports made it through," Nostro remarked.

"You think?" Wearl asked sarcastically.

Kalan scanned the battlefield. Jilla, Robin, Garcia and Flynn were all fighting the enemy. "Let's make them regret it."

Bob nudged his arm. "You sure you're all right, buddy? You're losing a lot of blood. Like, a *lot*."

Kalan smiled. "Don't worry. Us Grayhewns are hearty stock. I'll be fine."

Something caught his eye—a violent frenzy at the center of the battle. His grin widened as he looked closer. He should have known.

At the center of the raging battle stood Valerie, fighting a horde of angry Norruls.

That was exactly where Kalan wanted to be.

He pushed aside the strange dizzy feeling that threatened to overtake him and rushed into the battle.

The reached Valerie just as she was stabbing her sword into the gap in a Norrul's carapace and through its chest.

"Hey, boss. Need a hand?"

Valerie gave the wound on his face a concerned look, then glanced at the mass of Norruls around them. "Yeah. Let's get to work."

CHAPTER TWENTY

SSLAKE'S FORTRESS

While it would've been great to stop and ask Kalan why half his face was covered with blood, there was no time. Besides, it was pretty damn clear from the hordes of oncoming enemy fighters that it was far from over. Above the shield ships were going down—some crashing into it, others narrowly escaping—but Valerie was busy focusing on taking down enemy Norrul, one after another.

Other random enemies attacked too. She assuming they were escaped prisoners from SEDE, those who had survived the crash on Rhol and joined Demus. They were moving closer to the Sslake's chambers as they fought. Each strike Valerie blocked gave her a chance to glance at the building cautiously. She was worried that they'd infiltrate at any minute, and she and her team would be too late.

Kalan was tearing them up with shots one minute, turning to slam his elbow into an enemy the next, while

Jilla worked next to him. The two were knocking enemies back and forth as the invisible force that was Wearl finished others off from behind, unseen and deadly.

"There!" Robin shouted. A small army of robots was plowing through Skulla fighters, the tall form of Demus at their rear. He wasn't even bothering to attack; just gliding forward like a god, hands spread.

No, that wasn't right. He *was* attacking in a sense, just using his minions to do so. Even as she realized it ships came up from behind, filling friend and foe alike with bullets to clear his path. He was ruthless and evil, despite all the good he preached. His idea of justice meant calm *after* a storm that left millions or billions of dead in its wake.

That wasn't peace, and it sure as hell wasn't justice.

"Get me to him," Valerie seethed. She pushed past two Norrul in her path, tearing one's head from its body and throwing it at Demus. One of his ships blasted it apart before it hit, but the remains still splattered at the warlord's feet.

If Demus noticed, he wasn't fazed. He kept moving closer to Sslake's chambers.

At least Aranaught's mechs were engaging those ships now, so the damage was diverted from the Skulla ground troops.

Valerie turned to see three robots and a handful of Norrul almost on her. Where had they come from? She mowed down two of the Norrul and leaped for the robots, but they were too much for her.

Kalan plowed through them, shouting for her to go as he tore one robot apart and then used its remains to stab the remaining Norrul, even as others started to move in. Garcia unloaded, clearing a circle around them, while the others kept pushing toward Demus.

Valerie grabbed Kalan and pulled him over while Robin took his place to finish off his attackers. He caught his breath and nodded, then dove back into the fray.

He was a big boy, Valerie told herself, turning back to her target. Then she heard Jilla's shriek and the groan from Kalan. When she looked back there was an advanced Norrul with a bloodied metal horn in front of her, and stumbling back—and then collapsing—was Kalan.

"Kalan!" Valerie shouted, staring at him. She couldn't believe he'd fallen. There had already been a gash in one side of his face, but now there was a wound in his side as well. She turned and blocked a strike. No time to grieve now—and he was still moving, so he wasn't dead at least.

"No, no, no," Jilla cried, then turned to tear into the closest enemy. With so many attackers it was hard to tell which one had dealt the damage, but judging by Jilla's ferocity, she was holding all of them was responsible.

"Get him out of here!" Valerie shouted. Wearl began dragging him off, while Jilla and Bob took up defensive positions to keep him safe.

A new rage formed in Valerie, one that she had never been able to pull until something like this happened. She *pushed* fear as she let her fangs grow long and her eyes glow red, and then she charged.

It was a flurry of kicking and punching, slamming heads into the ground, sweeping enemy legs and grabbing their weapons to finish them off. Bullets flew, steel broke off into corpses, and blood splattered.

She didn't give a damn if there was a wall of enemies before her—she took them down one by one until she was running up a pile of corpses and leaping, bullets flying into her next round of victims. Then she landed, claws growing from her fingertips and she ran, not even slowing as she tore new foes to shreds.

The door to Sslake's chambers was open and there was a path of dead Skulla in Demus's wake. Valerie darted in, eyes searching.

"At last you've come to me," Demus's voice echoed throughout the chamber.

Valerie spun to attack, only to find herself surrounded by more of Demus's robots. They parted, and the high priest himself stepped forward. His cables reached out to connect to the robots and several of his Norrul generals nearby, and they all entered some sort of trance.

"They feed me, Prime Enforcer," he told her, holding out his arms as if expecting an embrace from her. "You must understand true power, if you hope to survive in this universe. You must come to see the light."

In a flash of metal and a brilliant blast of light he was in front of her, hands to her head. Again she was pulled out of herself, Demus's pulses of electricity messing with her mind, only his power was amplified by those connected to him.

The brightness cleared, and she was once again surrounded by purple fog. The dragon appeared, only this time she knew what to expect. This time she resisted, bringing it instead to her location of choice. She focused her mind on what could ground her, what could tell this sonofabitch that he had no dominion inside her head.

And then the fog and dragon were gone.

The sun shone warmly on her face. A breeze carried with it the scent of a cool spring day in Old Paris, where she'd been raised. She first saw the sparkling of the sunlight on the river, then her mother and father kneeling on a blanket and motioning for her to join them.

Nothing else. No sign of Demus…yet.

She approached, heart thudding and the corners of her eyes starting to glisten as she saw the faces of the parents she had nearly forgotten. They stared at her with such love that she felt the world couldn't contain it. This vision certainly couldn't.

So it was that when she turned to see Demus standing there, she wasn't worried. There was nothing he could do that could take this moment away from her. Even if they were long gone, the memory would be there forever. Their love always held her, reminded her of the woman she needed to be.

Demus took a step toward her, faceplate clear and eyes wide with confusion. Sorrow.

"Do not show me this place," he said, voice cracking. "You have no right!"

"This is what people like you destroy every day. I have every right."

He glared, breathing deeply as his ferocity took over. The faceplate clouded and he stepped forward—only he hesitated.

Valerie smiled, then looked to her side to see her friend Sandra standing there with her hand in Diego's. Two of her closest friends—the two she'd traveled with, arrived in America with. To her other side were the werewolf

Cammie and her vampire lover Royland. A glance back showed more friends there with her, some putting their hands on her shoulders while others took up attack positions. Every friend she could remember from Earth and her journey to reclaim honor—they were all there.

Of course, she knew they weren't. In the back of her mind she was aware that this was simply her way of overcoming any sort of power this Demus fuckhead though he could assert over her.

But not today. At that moment, she knew it wasn't only her body that was strong; her mind was too. Her mind, that had never been upgraded, never been changed by becoming a vampire or by slipping into a Pod-doc.

No, this was all her.

With a shout of victory, she led the charge. Sandra and the others at her side met Demus and his followers in a maelstrom of punches and kicks. Nothing he could throw at them did any damage, and every strike her side landed pushed him back or threw him down, until—

With a jolt, Valerie was back on Tol. Demus's hands were on her and his eyes were visible through his faceplate. He was staring at her in terror.

She grabbed his arms and kicked his torso harder than she'd ever kicked anything in her life. The first strike tore off one arm, and she clutched the other as she stomped on his leg and twisted. She pulled the other arm clean off, surprised to see that even his bones were metal, or were encased in it.

He turned to her, not to plead for his life or in fright. In pure anger he shouted, "I will destroy everything you love. I will—

His words were interrupted as she clubbed his head with his left arm. Her strikes came in hard, repeatedly, until his helmet cracked and fell apart. When he turned back, blood on his temple, she struck again until he appeared to not move.

"Not a single one of you will be alive after I—" he muttered, barely moving. She came at him in a barrage of strikes, using his arms like kali fighting sticks to rain blow after blow on him. His soldiers converged, robots and Norrul generals alike, but she wasn't stopping. Whack, whack...she took out two of his fighters, then got another couple whacks in on him before the next wave of jackasses required her attention.

Some landed blows on her, but she kept taking them down. She realized her armor couldn't take much more. Pieces shattered and others fell off, until soon she was left in her black uniform with its red stripes. She didn't care—it was easier to move this way; easier to dodge and strike.

It went on like this—whack whack for him, whack whack for them, and then soon she saw Robin and the others fighting toward her. Robin's expression changed from surprise to amusement when she saw what Valerie had done. Only then did Valerie realize there was a circle of defeated opponents around her, and a twitching Demus lay battered and bloody at her feet. His helmet had been destroyed; now he looked like any other defeated Norrul.

She dropped his arms and knelt beside him. "Nobody threatens those I care about. And you? You'll never hurt anyone ever again."

She grabbed the metallic horns that stuck out from his cheeks, bending them until they ripped out of his skin. He growled in pain and his eyes rolled up to meet hers, still filled with defiance and hatred.

There was only one way of stopping anyone like him, she knew, so she raised those metal horns and brought them down hard into his eyes, plunging them in as far as they'd go. She still wasn't sure it was done, so she stood and brought her foot down hard. The metal cut through his skull and lodged against the stone floor, and he no longer moved or breathed.

His side didn't have many survivors, but all within sight suddenly knelt in surrender. Robots collapsed to the ground, no longer connected.

Valerie and Robin turned to each other. They stumbled toward each other, then collapsed into each other's arms. They simply held each other, glad it was finally over.

EPILOGUE

PLANET TOL

Kalan woke with a start and his hand immediately went to his side, searching for his pistol.

He couldn't believe it; he'd passed out. They were in the middle of a battle, and Valerie needed him.

Instead of his pistol, his hand found a bandage and a soft sheet. He was in a bed. A hospital bed, it appeared.

Valerie stood next to the bed, arms crossed and a smile on her face. Bob and Jilla were there too. Mej and Lien stood on the other side of the bed, their tall orange forms bending down to look at him with concern on their faces.

"It would appear I missed a thing or two," he said hoarsely.

"Yeah, you did," Valerie confirmed. "We won. I had to kick Demus's ass without you."

Relief washed over him. "Is everyone okay?"

"Everyone but you," Bob answered.

Jilla glared at him. "Shut up, Bob!"

"I didn't mean it like that. It's just... His eye."

Kalan blinked, trying to understand. He suddenly realized that things looked different. Clearer, somehow.

"That Norrul spear caught you in the eye," Valerie explained. "The doctors had to take it out. Thankfully, Wearl got you to them in time."

Kalan's hand went to his eye socket. "I don't understand. I can see out of my right eye just fine. Better than before, actually."

Jilla chuckled. "Cybernetic eye. Wearl even helped them program it."

"Wow." Kalan wasn't sure how to respond to that. He was a cyborg, even if in a very minor way; he didn't know how he felt about that quite yet. For now, he'd try not to think about it. Instead, he turned to Mej and Lien. "How about your fleet? Did they come through okay?"

Mej nodded. "A few of their ships got through, as you undoubtedly noticed, but the ones who were dumb enough to stay and fight us learned what the Lavkin Fleet is all about."

"Now that they're taken care of, it's time for us to get on with what's next," Lien added. "Reuniting the rest of our fleet under Lolack. Finding the rest of the Bandians. Resuming our alliance."

Kalan chuckled. "If there *are* any other Bandians out there."

Mej smiled. "We believe there are, and we'd like you to help us find them."

"That... It would be amazing." Kalan turned to look at Valerie. "But I don't want to abandon the team."

Valerie smiled. "I think you should do it. Jilla and Bob

already said they're in if you are. You're all part of the Lavkin family now, after all. And we know Wearl would be up for it."

"Thank you. This means everything to me." He thought for a moment. "What about SEDE? With Tuttle gone, who's going to be in charge?"

Valerie chuckled. "Sslake put your buddy Nostro in charge, for now. Maybe permanently, if he can prove himself."

Kalan raised an eyebrow. "Nostro will be a good leader and captain, but is he qualified for that job?"

"Not even remotely. But he caught Sslake in a good mood after we saved his life again."

Now Kalan laughed. Knowing a fair leader was in charge of SEDE put his mind at ease. It meant things would get better for his mother, and that left Kalan free to pursue his destiny with the formerly Lost Fleet.

The Found Fleet. The one that would hopefully help him find the rest of his people.

He turned to Valerie. "There's something I want to say."

Valerie frowned. "You're not going to get all sappy on me, are you?"

"Incredibly sappy. You changed my life. Without you, I never would have met the Lavkins. I never would have learned that I'm a Bandian. I never would have found out the truth about myself."

She shrugged. "You would have figured it out."

"I don't think I would have. Besides, you taught me something else. Something even more valuable. You taught me what it means to fight for true justice. And I promise, no matter what happens, I'll never forget that lesson."

"I'll hold you to that," she said with a smile. "And I expect you to introduce me to the rest of your family once you find them."

"That I can do."

A noise in the doorway made him look up, and he saw a strange woman enter.

She was tall, almost Kalan's height, and her skin was a beautiful silver. Her hair was silver too, and it flowed with her every movement. Her eyes had no irises or pupils; they were orbs of silver that perfectly matched her skin and her hair.

Her steps were light as she moved across the room; she seemed to glide.

To Kalan, she was beautiful.

He'd never seen this female before, but something about her felt familiar.

Then the realization hit him. The cybernetic eye—the one Wearl had helped program.

"Hello, Kalan," she said. "You're looking hot, as usual."

He smiled. "Hello, Wearl. You're looking pretty good yourself."

Valerie felt horrible about Kalan's eye, but she knew she couldn't always protect everyone. She was still processing the fact that they had won; that Demus and all the enemy fleets that Aranaught had summoned before being altered were now either wiped out or had surrendered.

Losses had been monumental on both sides, but it was over.

Ironically, the peace and order that Demus had supposedly been fighting for might have been finally won by his demise.

"It's going to take a lot of work to clean all this up," Sslake said after thanking everyone for their help in this fight. Now Tol had the defensive system in place, so that if more attackers came they'd be safe. They also had so enough ship parts that they could build three new fleets, and many of them were surrendered enemy ships that could fix themselves. Add to that the fact that Lolack and Sslake had formed an official alliance, and that was a pretty good recipe for safety and security going forward.

A true ally for the Etheric Federation. One that would do its part to continue to keep this part of the universe safe.

"We're here to help," Valerie said.

"You have your own fight to get back to," Sslake replied.

"And yet, our ship was destroyed. It'll take some time to rebuild, but when it's ready—and maybe upgraded a bit— we'll contact our chain of command and see what they have in store for us."

"You're sure?" he asked.

Valerie glanced at Robin, who smiled and nodded.

"We could use a break from the chaos," Valerie admitted.

"Some down time," Robin added. "And then we'll go off to help save the rest of the universe."

"Exactly."

Sslake nodded, apparently not catching on to their tones or the smiles they were giving each other. He told one of his followers to show them to a house they could call their own while staying there, and soon they were checked in. Garcia and the others insisted they would get food and drink so the party could commence. After all, a victory like this demanded a celebration. Sleep, too, but that could wait.

"It's chaos out there," Valerie said from the balcony of the main room, looking out at the destruction. Smoke still rose from many of the fallen craft.

"Did you see the smiles on the Skulla's faces?" Robin said, approaching and leaning against that same rail. "They know they've won. That they have nothing to worry about for the foreseeable future."

"And you?" Valerie asked, turning and placing a hand on Robin's. "Are you sure you're okay with this?"

"As you said, we need the ship fixed up, and we need to recuperate so that when we get back out there, we're more badass than ever before."

"No, I meant..." She took the woman's hand in both of hers and kissed it. "With *this*."

Robin bit a lip and nodded. "I knew what you meant."

She moved her hand to the side of Valerie's face and through her hair, and then pulled her in for a kiss. Their lips met and Valerie melted into the moment, never wanting it to end.

Whatever came next, she was ready for it. Everything that was happening at that moment would just make her stronger. Make the two of them more powerful in their bond.

Ready to take on anything the universe threw their way.

I can't believe this makes sixteen books in the Kurtherian Gambit world for me! It's amazing that this series took me to the point where I was able to switch over to fulltime writing, leaving various other careers in the past.

Did you know that I had been a Marine, Presidential Management Fellow, Trade Specialist, Asia Analyst at the Federal Reserve Bank, Video Game Writer at Telltale Games, and Editor at Military.com? All of that fed into who I am and got me to this point. What a ride it's been!

And now I had the chance to bring you a snippet of Valerie's life. What do you think? I'd love to hear privately or in reviews. We first met her on her journey from France to America, and now she's up in space saving galaxies! With some help, of course. How'd you feel about Kalan? That was PT's baby, and I think it would be cool to see a Kalan spinoff. Thoughts?

And then there's the issue of Valerie's love life. I KNOW some readers aren't going to like how that ended. But you know what? It's the characters--we write them, and they take over. If I'd tried to force it some other direction, it would have felt unnatural. Vampires, by the way, have often kind of transcended human ideas of love and relationships, so maybe if you didn't like it, just shrug it off as a vampire thing. Lol. If you liked it, or loved it—great!

What's next for me? Outside of the KGU, I recently published my Biotech Wars trilogy. It's complete, but guess what? It set up my next series--the Ascension Gate series. This is the massive, just me (solo) series that I've been outlining with my wife for a year. It's going to be huge. A sort of "Stargate meets Dragon Riders of Pern." And the main bad guy... When you meet him, you'll see why I can say he puts Thanos to shame. Pssh.

So I hope you'll check out those series! If you love Space Marines, crazy battles, and dragons, you'll be a great fit.

Before I go, I need to say a humongous thank you to everyone who has helped along the way! Lynne has done an amazing job editing most of these books, and I've also worked with Candy, Calee, and Stephen on earlier books. All of you readers have been amazing, especially those of you who have joined my on my Facebook group, THE SLOAN ZONE and continue to read my other books. That's an amazing feeling! All of you have been such an inspiration for me. Of course, a big thanks to Michael Anderle for taking me into this world, Craig Martelle for kicking butt with the Age of Expansion, and for CM Raymond and LE Barbant for their help in the Age of Magic.

I don't know if I've told you all how I actually got involved in this in the first place, did I? It was funny, actually – Michael Scott Earle gave me the idea, and then I reached out to Michael Anderle and he was super cool about it. I say funny, because then the Earle book that he was preparing at the same time ended up going off to be his Star Justice series. Crazy how these things can change along the way, and what a role friendships can play in our careers.

All that said, who knows where these crazy writing lives will take us next. I hope you stick with me for the journey.

Thank you again for coming on this wild ride with us!

Justin

It was almost exactly a year ago today—on my thirty-ninth birthday—that I got a text from Michael asking if I'd be interested in writing in the KGU. I thought about it for all of twelve seconds before responding.

Shortly after that I started talking with CM Raymond and LE Barbant, planning my Age of Magic series. And about six months later Justin asked me if I'd be interested in helping him take Valerie into space.

The world of writing is a weird, wonderful, and truly strange place.

A big thanks to Michael for taking a chance on me and letting me write in his universe. A big thanks to Justin for letting me tag along on this phase of Valerie's journey. And a big thanks to Craig Martelle for shepherding this series and the Age of Expansion.

And, as always, a giant thanks to Steve, Lynne, and the JIT team. Y'all are the magic that makes these books shine.

The most amazing thing I've gotten out of the experience of writing in the KGU is the connections with readers. Someone mentioned on Facebook the other day that *Storm Raiders* was their first Kurtherian Gambit book and they've since gone through and read every book in the universe. I was blown away. Then another reader commented that *Storm Raiders* was their gateway drug to the universe as well.

Honestly, that was a powerful moment for me. It felt great to know I've helped bring some new readers into this universe that has done so much for my writing career.

So what's next for me? The Vampire World Saga is my current obsession/project. The first two books are out now, and the third is dropping May 10th. These books are non-stop action, and good old fashion fun. I hope you check them out.

Will Kalan be back? I hope so. I've got some plans for him to pop up, though maybe not in the place you think. I'm psyched for you to see what I've got cooking...

If you'd like to stay connected with me, check out my Facebook group The Hylton Reader. It's weird in there. In a good way.

Thanks for reading!

PT

BOOKS BY MICHAEL ANDERLE

Sign up for the LMBPN email list to be notified of new releases and special deals!

https://lmbpn.com/email/

For a complete list of books by Michael Anderle, please visit:

www.lmbpn.com/ma-books/